THE
BRIGHT
SIDE
OF THE
MOON

THE
BRIGHT
SIDE
OF THE
MOON

CINDY BARNETT

Cover design created by Rachelle Chibitty

Author photo by Audrey Barnett

Printed in the United States of America

Publishing services by Selah Publishing Group, LLC, Tennessee. The views expressed or implied in this work do not necessarily reflect those of Selah Publishing Group.

This is a work of fiction, although Remington does exist in northern Indiana, and a few actual place names and facts are included. The Remington of this story is fiction. Names, characters, places and incidents either are products of the author's imagination or are used fictitiously. Any resemblance to actual events or locales or persons, living or dead, is entirely coincidental.

ISBN: 978-1-58930-296-9
Library of Congress Control Number:2014920630

ACKNOWLEDGEMENTS

Thank you to Alexa Taylor and Diana Barnett for reading my manuscript and offering suggestions and encouragement. Thank you to my husband, Jeff Barnett, for listening to me talk about this project for the many years it took to complete.

The little town of Remington does exist in northern Indiana, and I have included a few factual details, but the Remington of this story is fiction.

Other books by this author:
Never Far from Home

CHAPTER 1

October 1938
Sunday

DANNY MCCOOL FELL FROM THE SKY INTO THE WALSTRA CORNFIELD on an otherwise normal Sunday evening. In the farmhouse below, Mary Walstra washed, little Rita dried, Ellen put each dish away while the curtains billowed inward over the dishpan.

Mary stared out the window, hands scrubbing plates by instinct. The sky appeared to be split in two; air glowing gold where the sun disappeared into the cornfield, dark folds of clouds edging in from the south. She paused, leaning toward the open window.

"Russell," Mary called toward the sitting room. "Come look at this sunset."

"Just saw it when I was outside."

"No, it's changed. The colors are so vivid and it looks like a storm coming in."

And then she saw the airplane. It shuddered overhead, made a low looping circle, and glided just above the cornfield beyond the barn.

"Russell! An airplane. I think it's going to crash."

She watched the plane as it drifted toward the ground, disappeared, bounced up and down twice, and finally came to rest, one wing poking above the cornstalks like a banner. By this time Russell was outside, headed toward the car.

Ellen and Rita stood at the door, faces pressed against the window. Mary stretched her arms around them as they watched Russell pushing and pulling levers in the Model A, shaking it to life.

Ellen reached for the doorknob. "Can I go?"

"Oh my, no," Mary said. "We have no idea…"

They watched the car bump down the farm road while dark clouds spread overhead.

Wind gusts twirled the weather vane and rain pattered on the roof by the time the car returned. Mary watched as Russell and a man in startling white shoes, leather jacket, and aviator's cap helped a young woman out of the car and then supported her between them as they walked toward the house.

"You better call Dr. Mendel," Russell said as they stepped through the door.

The little procession moved past her into the next room as she grasped the black candlestick phone and called the doctor. When she joined the others, the woman was slumped onto the davenport, limp as a Raggedy Ann doll. The aviator batted at the blood on his white shirt before turning to face the Walstra family, the leather flaps on his cap dangling like the ears of a coon dog.

"Well," he announced. "My name is Danny McCool, and this lovely woman is Jean Swanson, my fiancée." He swept his arm toward Jean, who narrowed her eyes like a cornered animal and then turned her face away.

Dr. Mendel arrived within the hour. "Cuts and bruises, probably a neck sprain," he said after his examination. "Get some rest, keep the cuts clean." He stepped aside and spoke quietly to Russell and Mary. "The worst thing is the mental shock to this little lady." He nodded toward Jean, who lay quietly on the davenport, eyes staring at the ceiling. He placed his stethoscope in his bag, laid a packet of aspirin on the table, and left.

Mary unfolded a thin quilt and spread it over Jean, tucking it under her feet. Jean's eyes looked past Mary to the aviator, who stood at the end of the davenport. "My father's going to kill you, flying down here, doing your tricks."

"It wasn't tricks. We had some engine trouble, you know." He looked into the faces of the Walstra family, who stood in a silent semicircle around him. "Please excuse her, she's a little excitable."

"I am not excitable," she said, raising her head from the pillow. She quickly lay back down. "My neck hurts."

"The doctor said you probably have a neck sprain." He spoke slowly, as to a child.

"Of course I have a neck sprain." Her voice rose again. "Bouncing up and down, hitting the ceiling of that plane. All because of you."

"Jean, dear, we landed safely. Everything's going to be all right." He reached out to her but she pushed his hand away.

"Call my father."

Mr. McCool turned toward Russell. "Do you folks have a phone?"

"Sure, help yourself," Russell said. He pointed toward the kitchen.

Mary remembered the comforting power of food. "I'm sure you two are hungry," she said. "Ellen, go out to the meat shed and cut off some ham."

"Sounds wonderful," said the aviator. "I am famished, now that you mention it."

Jean turned her head and smiled up to Mary. "Thank you, dear. I'd love some hot coffee. I'm sorry about all this trouble Danny has caused."

Mary said, "Don't worry. You just rest."

Ellen returned from the shed with a slab of ham the size of a small book, which Mary placed in a frying pan on the woodstove. She took bread from the bread box and cut thick slices. She heated water for coffee.

Mr. McCool's voice rang out behind her as he spoke into the phone.

"We're both fine."

"No, the engine."

"Whatever you say, sir."

"I'd say about a hundred miles south of Chicago."

He lowered his voice. "Russell, what town are we near?"

"Remington, Indiana, south of Renesselaer," Russell said. "Just ask for Russ Walstra and anyone in town can tell him how to get here."

He repeated the information into the phone. "Okay, see you tomorrow."

Mary returned to the sitting room, where little Rita knelt by Jean, running her hand over the fabric of her dress. "Where did you get this pretty dress?" Rita asked.

"Now, don't wear her out, Rita." Mary couldn't help but notice the fine dress, though. A purple print, like purple ladybugs, with a white collar, belted at the waist. The woman must be used to fine things.

"Rita, go get some bread and coffee for Jean."

Rita carried the plate into the sitting room, placing it on a table by the davenport. She put her arm around Jean's shoulders to help her sit up and then held out the bulky white cup of black coffee.

Jean took a tiny bite from the bread and a tentative sip from the cup, steam rising in front of her face. "This is delicious, dear."

"I helped Mother make the jam this summer. I'm seven, so she lets me help."

Mary smiled at little Rita, who had the situation under control, and returned to the kitchen. She turned over the ham in the skillet while Ellen set a plate and silverware on the table. Russell pulled out a chair and motioned for the aviator to sit down. Ellen sat down across from him, arms folded on the table, watching their guest as he scooped butter onto a slice of bread.

"Did you know Amelia Earhart?" Ellen asked, leaning forward, eyes bright.

"Now, just because he flies a plane, see, doesn't mean…" Russell said.

Mr. McCool raised his brows and looked at Ellen. "You know, I did meet her down at Lafayette."

Mary forked the ham, still sizzling, onto the aviator's plate. "We're going to thank the Lord," she said.

Mr. McCool put down his knife and bowed his head. Everyone stopped where they were and bowed their heads. Mary looked to Russell.

Russell took off his hat. "Father God, thank You for landing this plane safely in our field without any real harm to Mr. McCool or Jean. We thank You for this food You have bountifully provided. In Jesus' name, amen."

As soon as the prayer ended, Ellen continued, "So, did you talk to Amelia Earhart? What was she like?"

"Well, I was there at the lecture she gave. At the university in 1935. It was all about women, about pursuing careers." He looked 'round the table and smiled. "Just another case of where I seem to be at the right place at the right time." He took a bite of ham and went on. "She looked quite dashing, wore men's trousers, but always a nice silk scarf around her neck. All the women wanted to be like her."

Mary pushed her chair back with a loud scrape on the floor, interrupting the man's discussion, and walked to the cupboard. "I forgot the cream." She carried the pitcher to the table and set it down.

"A shame what happened to her, lost at sea and all," Russell said. "Seems like maybe she took too many chances, took things a little too far."

Mr. McCool reached for the cream. "Who's to say? But look at all the things she accomplished. I daresay more than I ever will, and a woman at that." He winked at Ellen. "But you never know. I may fly across the Atlantic someday."

"Well, let's see about getting you out of the field first," Russell said.

"Got a point there." Danny raised his cup as if in a toast, then tipped it up and drained it. He backed his chair from the table, stood up, and bent forward in a deep bow before Ellen and Mary.

"My compliments to the cooks," he said. Ellen giggled and turned to Mary, who wiped her hands on her apron and began clearing the dishes. Russell shook his head at Mary and stood up.

Mr. McCool pulled a deck of playing cards from his back pocket, shuffled them in a blur, and fanned them out in front of Ellen. "Pick a card, any card." Ellen looked up to Mary as if to get permission and then picked up one of the cards.

Russell nodded his head toward Mary and then away from the table. She frowned as she followed him up the stairs in the dark.

"What are we going to do with these people?" Russell asked.

CHAPTER 2

Spring 1968

I LIKE TO READ MYSTERIES. THEY START WITH A PUZZLING SITUATION, then clues and obstacles and danger follow, but eventually everything turns out all right and it all makes sense. So far, my own life wasn't making sense. I needed change. I needed something, I just wasn't sure what. And then a new family moved into the area on the warmest day of spring break, April ninth. It was exactly one year and one month after Mom died. Other things happened later, but this was the beginning.

I was sitting on a blanket, reading and sunning myself at Aunt Rita's house in the country. I often ended up there since Dad had to work, I was only eleven, and my older brother, Marty, wasn't any help. Looking over the top of my Hardy Boys mystery, *The Disappearing Floor,* I saw a car stop at the little brick church building about a half mile down the straight-as-a-ruler county road. Several people got out of the car and walked up to the abandoned building.

I pulled on my cousin's arm. "Lana, look. We have a situation."

Lana lay flat on the blanket beside me, arms out, pale face to the sun. I laid my book upside-down on the grass, ran to the house, and returned with Uncle Phil's telescope. I unfolded the tripod and pointed the scope down the road.

"You shouldn't spy on people like that, Jude."

"They can't see me. I want to know what's going on."

I twisted the focus knob and then gave the report.

"They're from Kentucky."

"How you know that?"

"Kentucky license plates on a blue Dodge. Looks like a mom with two daughters and a baby. They're unloading stuff into the church. Boxes. A high chair. Looks like they're moving in."

"How're they going to live in that old church building?"

"I don't know," I said slowly, watching them through the scope. "I think we have a real-life mystery here."

Lana lay back down on the blanket and closed her eyes.

Over the next few days we rode our bikes back and forth by the church. The car was still there. Trash burned in a pile out back. They were definitely living there.

Lana explained the situation to Aunt Rita, who stood in the kitchen, apron on, cooking as usual.

"We'll be a good neighbor," she said, placing a stack of freshly made Rice Krispie treats on a paper plate. "You can take these down to them."

We placed the treats in the basket of Lana's bicycle and pedaled to the church. I led the way up the steps, holding the plate high in my left hand like a waiter, and knocked on the door. A woman opened the door a few inches, like she wasn't dressed or she wanted to hide something.

"Hi, these are for you since you just moved in. From my aunt." I held out the plate.

"Don't be thinking we need your help," she said. She looked past us to see if we were alone. "We're doing just fine." She didn't smile but opened the door a little wider and took the plate.

Two girls stepped up behind her, filling the doorway so I still couldn't see inside. The older one, who looked to be about eighteen, was holding a baby. They all stared at us, faces blank. There was nothing else to say so we left.

"They didn't seem too happy," Lana said as we got on our bikes.

I kept thinking of the girls' blank, sad faces as we drove home. I remembered that sad, blank feeling myself.

People said our family was doing better, but some days it didn't feel like it. There were some things we just avoided, or things we didn't say. We wouldn't travel down a certain stretch of State Road 231, I wouldn't look at the thin crescent moon, I dreaded my birthday. But Dad would explain, "It's like when someone has to overcome their fear of riding after being thrown by a horse. They just have to get back on the horse and ride it." Then we'd do something that was supposed to help us move on.

We did drive down State Road 231 once or twice, and I did have my birthday. But mostly we "stayed busy," which is what people said was the best thing to do. Sometimes that was hard in a small, boring town. There wasn't much to do and nothing exciting happened. Things were happening in the rest of the world. On TV, all the talk was about Vietnam and the anti-war demonstrations. There was the civil rights movement and then Martin Luther King's assassination. But nothing much happened in Remington.

Lana and I counted down the days until summer vacation, as rains came and winds blew across our flat northern Indiana fields. The most excitement we had was the day we were almost hit with a tornado. It was the middle of May, warm and breezy all afternoon. I was in the kitchen after school when I heard tornado warnings on the radio. I went to the porch, looking past the trees that were swaying in the wind to the dark clouds in the southwest. Dad was trying to shut the big door on the garage, yanking it back and forth because it was stuck.

"There's tornado warnings," I shouted.

"Get back in the house," he said with his irritated voice.

I walked down the steps into the yard. "I just want to watch—" I started to say, when a plastic Easter bunny from the Kaminskys' yard slammed against my leg on a gust of wind.

"Get back in the house," he said. He grabbed my arm and we ran together up the steps into the house.

My brother, Marty, was watching the news. "There's a tornado warning," he said.

"We're going to the basement," Dad said, "C'mon."

"Can't we watch out the windows and just go down at the last minute?" I asked.

Dad walked into the kitchen, looked out the kitchen window at the Kaminskys' flag whipping in the wind in all directions, trees swaying overhead.

"It looks like now would be a good time."

We went down the stone steps to the little square room that was our basement. We stood on the cracked cement floor next to dust-covered boxes and shelves. I tried to see through the little rectangular window near the ceiling, but could only see shifting shadows. We could hear the wind and creaking sounds of the old house. I began to feel afraid. What if a tornado really blew the house down? Would the floor collapse, or would we be sucked out, or lose all our possessions? I crouched on the floor close to Dad.

"We'll be fine down here," he said. After a while, it seemed quieter so we went back upstairs. It turned out the tornado went south of us, just north of Lafayette. A few limbs came down in the yard. The Kaminskys had to search the neighborhood for all their holiday decorations that blew away, but there was no real damage.

I guess it was a conundrum that I wanted to see a tornado but was afraid that I actually would.

The two girls we saw in that church building never did show up at school that spring. Finally, May 28 came. We cleaned out our fifth-grade desks, picked up our report cards, and poured out through the double doors at the last bell.

"Hey, Jude, see you next year. Hey, Jude. Hey, Jude." Ever since the Beatles came out with "Hey Jude," only teachers and adults called me Judy anymore. I liked it; it made me feel popular.

Lana got on the school bus and I joined up with my neighbor Trudy Kaminsky to walk the six blocks home. Trudy opened her report card.

"Mostly Cs, one D, a B in PE, but who cares, I'm a freshman!" A smile lit up her round face. "How about you?"

I peeked into the envelope. I realized I'd slipped a little this year.

"Four As, two Bs," I told her. I slid the card back into the envelope.

"Geez," she said.

We passed under maple trees in full leaf, down a sidewalk lined with bright green lawns. The warm air trailed around us, smooth on our skin.

"What a halcyon day," I said.

"A what? Where'd you get that word?"

"From a book I read. It means calm and peaceful."

Trudy twirled her finger by her ear. "You're crazy, Jude."

Trudy was one of the few who treated me like a normal person after Mom died.

I liked using words like *halcyon* or *oxymoron* or *conundrum*, even though I was the only girl my age who did. I would add a big word to a sentence to spice it up. I learned new words by reading, by spending whole afternoons hunched over the little round table in the library as a kid. I loved the smell of the new books with their fresh plastic covers, and the old ones patched with yellowed tape. Mom taught me to read before I even started school, and she knew a lot about books because she used to work at the library. She said a story can take you anywhere. I liked that, because I wanted to go places. Since she died, I started reading even more because it helped fill up my mind and forget she wasn't there.

On the first day of summer vacation, Aunt Rita brought Lana to my house to spend the weekend. We walked across town to the Caboose Café. The only other places to eat in Remington were Woody's Snack Shop, which was the teenage hangout downtown, and Shooter's Bar, which was obviously off-limits to us. The Caboose Café was attached to a real caboose from the TP&W Railroad, painted red with yellow trim, bright as a Lionel toy train. It stood at the edge of town next to the grain elevator and Texaco gas station.

Lana and I climbed the steps between beds of daisies and petunias hemmed in with railroad ties. Lana placed her hand on top of the TP&W Railroad marker that flanked the door.

"What's TP&W mean, anyway?" she asked.

"Toledo, Peoria, and Western Railroad. That's the railroad that goes through town, straight west to Peoria, Illinois," I said.

The tracks literally ran down the middle of the main street of town, which was why it was named Railroad Street.

"I don't know where it goes after that, maybe all the way to California," I added.

We walked through the Caboose with its postcard rack and shelves of souvenirs, down the short connecting hallway to the actual restaurant, and slid into a booth. I looked over the plastic-covered menu and told the waitress, "We'll just have two Cokes, one cherry and one vanilla. And fries. And ketchup."

I looked across the table at Lana. "You're lucky you have red hair," I said. "It stands out. It's your prominent feature."

"Are you kidding? I hate it. You're lucky."

"I don't think so. My only good feature is my eyes. Trudy says they're shocking blue." I lifted a limp strand of my hair. "My hair is just ordinary brown." I thought of my mother's thick, almost black hair and her blue eyes.

"At least your hair is straight. I'd have to iron mine to get it straight. Stephanie irons hers."

"Can you actually iron hair?"

"Yeah, I know girls that do. Just put their hair on the ironing board and iron it. You got to be careful, though."

I took off my jacket and spread it over the back of the red vinyl seat just as Trudy walked up to our table. Her straight black hair came from the Miami Indian ancestors on her mom's side.

"I yelled at you guys outside, but you didn't hear me." She sat down by Lana.

"Look at these pennies," she said. She held out three copper disks, flattened to a thin oval. "Yesterday, Spike showed me and Julie how you can put pennies on the railroad tracks and let the trains run over them. They get squashed like this and then you can put a hole in them and wear them like a necklace."

"My mom said not to do that. It could cause the train to crash," Lana said.

"That's what I told Spike, but he said it would just be like a car running over a bug. Even if you put down hundreds of pennies or even nickels or quarters."

She pulled a necklace from inside her blouse and held it out from her neck. A thin elongated quarter dangled from the end. "Spike gave this to me." She smiled and held her head a little higher.

"I don't know," Lana said. "It seems like it could wreck a train, maybe." When Trudy's face started to fall, she added, "But that's a nice necklace."

"Are you and Spike going steady?" I asked. Trudy was fourteen and always a step ahead of us.

"Sort of."

"Do your dad and mom know?"

"'Course not." She dropped the necklace back down inside her shirt and pushed her heavy black hair behind her ears.

Trudy Kaminsky wasn't a bad girl, but her parents were easily upset. I guess you could say they had volatile personalities. They seemed like an odd combination. He was Polish with a bald head and compact body; she was a Miami Indian, slightly taller, with luscious black hair. Trudy told me that one time her dad took all the doors off the hinges and stored them in the garage because he got tired of her slamming a door every single time she got mad. They had no doors for five months, except her mom and dad's bedroom door. A blanket covered the opening to the bathroom.

Another time, her mother threw dishes, good ones, against the wall, smashing them to bits, when Mr. Kaminsky accused her of being just like her mother. Their family knew how to make a point. Since they lived next door to us, we often heard loud noises and would look through the blinds to see one of her brothers leave the house and take off down the street or some other dramatic thing.

It had been a little quieter since her brother Steven went to Vietnam and they put the gold star in their window.

We finished our food and Trudy left.

I laid down a quarter for a tip and paid the bill.

"By the way, where'd you get all this money?" Lana asked.

"Grandma's going to start paying me for helping her. She says since I'm growing up I need a little spending money. But it's not much."

We walked down the wooden sidewalk in front of the caboose, and I laid two shiny pennies on the railroad tracks.

We returned to the house and watched TV all afternoon. Summer seemed to lie before us like an unending road. After supper we rode our bikes around Remington until the setting sun cast an orange glow over the town. Even our ordinary white house, ordinary except for the gingerbread designs under the front gable, had taken on a golden hue. We laid our bikes on the ground by the peonies with their pink blooms that looked like giant corsages. My brother, Marty, was sitting in the porch swing, a column of Oreos in one hand, a glass of milk in the other.

"Hey, Jude, Dad got us some Oreos but they're all gone."

I knew he was lying to me, as usual. Dad would have saved some for me. I crossed the porch and punched him. Marty whirled back at me, unbalancing his glass of milk, sending splatters across his pants. I stepped aside and ran into the house, where Dad was watching *Bonanza* from his brown chair where he always sat.

"There's some cookies for you in the kitchen," he said.

"I knew it," I told Lana and then turned to Dad. "Do you know about those people that moved into that old church building?"

"Nope."

He was done talking, so we went to the kitchen. There were Oreos on the table. I filled two plastic glasses with iced tea and handed the bag of Oreos to Lana. We climbed two sets of stairs to the third-story attic, our secret hideaway. Our house wasn't that big but it was tall. The attic stairs led off from my bedroom, so I could go up there any-time. I didn't mind going up in the daytime, but after dark I never went up alone because, I hate to admit, I was a little scared. Once I scared myself with my own reflection in a mirror that was stored up there, so I kept it covered with an old blanket.

A window looked out north and south from the oblong room with its steep sloping walls. The attic also extended off to the east over the kitchen where a third window overlooked the Kaminskys' backyard. Boxes of clothes, business papers, and so forth were placed in unor-ganized stacks next to antique chairs and other furniture. Grandma and Grandpa James stored their furniture with us when they moved to a smaller house in Tennessee. I formed narrow paths to get around.

Lana and I settled into two old stuffed chairs by the north window and set our drinks on a wooden trunk.

"I'm so glad school's out." I slapped my arms on the chair sending dust into the air.

"I know. We can do whatever we want."

I stood and pushed open the window. Lana and I leaned on the windowsill, our heads extended into the warm air.

"Pretty soon it'll be too hot to come up here," I said.

The wind swished the tree leaves below us. I looked out the window toward the center of Remington, where I could see past the housetops to the few stores that lined Railroad Street. If I watched long enough, I would see a freight train coming down the tracks. I could see the neon lights from the Caboose Cafe and the Texaco gas station on the other side of the railroad tracks. The grain elevator with its silos and grain bins loomed nearby. Beyond that was farming country, corn and soybean fields stretching almost forever in neat squares like a patchwork quilt on land as flat as the floor of a house.

Spots of light confirmed where farmhouses stood along the roads. Moving dots of lights represented cars. I couldn't actually see all this from my window, but I imagined it would look this way from an airplane. Dad said I had a vivid imagination. There were months last year when I had no imagination at all, when I felt like a blank piece of paper. But my imagination was back again after a little time off. Maybe things really were getting better.

"Someday I'm going to fly," I said to Lana.

"Like Superman?" Sometimes Lana seemed a little slow to me.

"No, of course not. Maybe I'll be a pilot. Or an astronaut." We walked around boxes to the east window, which I opened wide. The sky was clear. "There's the constellation Leo," I pointed out. "It's shaped like a lion, and that orange star underneath it is Mars." It looked orange next to the whiteness of the almost-full moon hanging just above the Kaminskys' house. "You can sort of make out a man's face in the moon, see? The dark areas are formed by the lunar seas."

Lana listened, but I knew she didn't care. Uncle Phil was the only one in the family who knew the constellations like me. It was one thing I had in common with him.

Lana took in a deep breath. "I can smell your lilacs."

"I know, it's intoxicating. Luxurious."

We pulled the chain hanging from the single light bulb and used a flashlight to find our way down the dark staircase. My imagination got going.

The young girls held the candle before them as they descended into the basement where possible danger waited. The air was foul and oppressive. Water dripped from the ceiling. They came to the door and stood in anticipation. They heard someone on the other side. They gathered up their courage and threw open the door.

Dad stood at the bedroom door. "Hey, time for you two to get to bed."

Dad was doing the best he could. Right after Mom died, he sat down with me and Marty and said, "We're going to have to be patient with each other and work together like a team. It's just us now. We're a team."

Marty and I sat on the plaid couch across from Dad in his brown chair. He looked back and forth from me to Marty. It was a solemn time, and we both agreed to be a part of the team and do our share. We reached out our right hands and joined them together, like we were sealing a pact or pumping each other up before a big game.

Now, a year later, I felt like I was doing my part. I could fix supper and wash dishes by myself. Dad bought all the groceries and did some of the cooking. Hamburgers, egg sandwiches, hot dogs, that kind of thing. Sometimes Aunt Rita and Grandma Walstra dropped off a casserole or a pie to help out.

I was the main one who did the laundry and tried to keep the house clean. Grandma Walstra gave me a few tips, showed me how to use scouring powder to clean the sinks, how to divide the laundry into different groups and how much Tide to use. Whenever she came to our house, the first thing she did was check the bathrooms and kitchen. By the time she left, the house smelled bright and clean. But Dad kept reminding us we were a team and had to learn to get by on our own. Maybe he thought Marty would get the idea better if he used a sports term, but it seemed like the only thing Marty did was take out the trash. He did work at the A&P stocking shelves during the summer, but that would end when basketball practice started. At least Marty didn't expect us to wait on him hand and foot like Mom always did. Dad made him fix his own sandwiches and told him he was perfectly able to open a can of soup.

Sunday afternoon Lana and I went back to the tracks and looked for our pennies. We found them both, well smashed, in the rocks a few feet away from where we'd placed them. We also found a black mitten.

"Now, that is serendipity," I said.

"What?"

"It's when you're looking for one thing and by fortunate accident you find something wonderful you're not looking for."

"So what's so wonderful about one mitten?"

"Nothing that we know of, not yet anyway. But that's what serendipity means. And the mitten could be a clue to a mystery."

I placed the black mitten in my briefcase and buttoned up my trench coat against the cold. I would take the evidence down to Headquarters. I crossed the tracks looking both ways for any suspicious activity and decided to take an alternate route home.

Lana was my best friend but sometimes she got on my nerves. One Saturday morning we sat at the kitchen table eating cereal in our pajamas. It was eleven o'clock.

"Is Uncle R.J. going to get another job?" Lana asked.

"He's got a job. He's a mechanic. You know that. He gets other jobs, too." I was irritated with her.

We both looked out the window at the cars lining the driveway and the three cars with "For Sale" on their windshields parked in a short row by the street.

"He's going to have his own shop. He's been talking to Uncle Max."

"But it's been like two years now," she said, stirring her cereal 'round and 'round.

I remembered that day two years ago. It was the first time I heard Mom and Dad really argue. They weren't like the Kaminskys; they usually kept their feelings more to themselves. Dad walked in the door and told Mom point-blank, "Ellen, I'm not working at the elevator anymore."

"What do you mean?" She put a lid on the pot of potatoes and turned the heat down. "Did they lay you off for the winter?"

"I quit."

"What do you mean, you quit?" She sat down at the table.

"I mean, I quit." His voice was raised.

Mom dried her hands with the kitchen towel, over and over, until she saw me standing in the doorway.

"Judy, go on and play outside. I'll call you in for supper."

"Go on, Blue Jay," Dad said quietly.

I walked loudly through the living room, opened and shut the front door, then circled quietly back through the room and stood hidden behind the open kitchen door. I could see through the narrow crack.

"I've been thinking about it a long time. And I finally got the courage to do it."

"Courage? That's not courage. That's stupidity," Mom said.

"You don't know what it's like, working for Harold Hoagland."

"That's ridiculous. Courage would be to stay there, even if it was hard. What are we going to do for money? What's your courage going to do?"

"Okay, stop saying the word *courage*." He hit the table with his hand. His voice got quiet again. "Ellen, I did this so we could have more money."

"Of course, now we'll have all the money we need." She threw one arm up like she was tossing a ball in the air and rolled her eyes.

"Ellen, listen. You know I'm never going to get ahead working at the grain elevator. The only way to get ahead is to have your own business."

"The grain elevator paid the bills."

"You know I've always had odd jobs on the side, and I've been talking to Max. He said there's good money in car repair. I know how to fix cars, that's what I used to do, remember? Back when I worked for Devore?" Mom stood listening, rolling and twisting the towel in her hands. "I can start out in the garage. Then maybe Max and I could go in together, buy a building. And sell cars, too. It makes me feel good to think about it. I could be my own boss. I can keep getting other jobs on the side, repair work, painting."

"What about the bills next week? You don't get any money being a volunteer fireman."

"Well, we've got your money from the library."

"That's not much."

I peeked around the door. I thought I smelled the potatoes beginning to scorch.

Dad stood across the table from Mom. She looked out the window like she was about to cry. He put on his coat and went outside.

I walked into the kitchen, moved the pan of potatoes off the burner, and turned it off. Mom didn't seem to notice me.

Lana and I put our bowls in the sink, dressed, and headed out the back door to feed the cat. We were on our way to the school to play tetherball, dressed in summer shorts and tank tops.

Mr. Kaminsky stood next to his shed, holding a plastic reindeer under each arm. He was short but Dad said he was "strong as an ox." He worked for the highway department and used to be in the army. He reminded me of an aging wrestler.

"Getting ready for Christmas, Mr. Kaminsky?"

"Not yet. Just rearranging Halloween and Christmas, looking for my Fourth of July flags."

Lana and I called the Kaminskys' home the "Holiday House." They were the ones who always tried to outdo everyone else at Christmastime. Their home blazed with thousands of lights, colored and white, flashing and non-flashing. If we turned off our electricity in December, we could read by the light from their house. They decorated for every single holiday as if they were trying to win a contest. Two gazing balls, gnomes in the flower bed, and a plastic deer family stayed up year-round.

Dad said, "There's always one in every town."

The Kaminskys weren't the only odd ones in town. On our way to the school, we slowed down at Old Herb Hoagland's house and looked between the dense bushes that surrounded his unpainted house. He lived alone and wasn't able to take care of his place because he had a fake leg and only half of his right hand since his fall at the grain elevator. He could barely get around. Kids said he was crazy. All I knew was that Dad said he and his brother, Harold, were hard to work for and he didn't want to talk about it.

I saw Old Herb sitting on his back steps in the sun. His wooden leg stood up beside him like an extra-tall cowboy boot in the tall grass. He had his pants leg rolled up, and I could see the pink end of the stump of his leg. Leather straps hung down from the top of the artificial leg.

"Maybe he's airing it out," I said, "but it's weird." We hurried on.

I beat Lana in nine out of ten tetherball games. As we walked back home from the school, we went over the names we'd given to the houses in town. There was Old Herb's *Crazy House*; there was the *House with All the Kids*, where the Antorettis lived with their seven small children; the *Music House*, where everyone in the family played an instrument; the *Ugly House*, which was a funny purplish color; the Kaminskys' *Holiday House*; the modern *Glass House*; the *Rock House,* made entirely of rocks; the *Haunted House*; and so on.

"And don't forget the *Church House*," Lana added.

"That's right. We'll have to add it to our list."

As my own house came into view, I counted the cars in the front yard and wondered what name people gave to our place. *The House with All the Junk Cars?* Funny how I hadn't really seen it that way before.

CHAPTER 3

October 1938
Monday

MARY ADDED WOOD TO THE KITCHEN STOVE UNTIL IT HUMMED with heat. This time of year she was up long before the sun appeared behind the four apple trees they called The Orchard. The morning star glowed in the east, a sliver of moon hanging below like a crooked smile.

The visitors had stayed the night. Jean remained on the flowered davenport, and Danny McCool slept on the daybed in the closed-in front porch. Mary and Russell stood at the top of the stairs the night before while their girls laughed in the kitchen below with this total stranger, spellbound by his card tricks.

"Russell, you know I have so much to do this time of year, and circumstances being what they are…" She was not one to take in boarders; neither of them were.

"Jean's father will be coming for her, and we'll see about fixing that plane," Russell said. "I'm no happier about it than you are." He placed his hand, thick and rough from farmwork, on her shoulder.

"We know nothing about these people," she said.

"We have no choice."

It was after midnight before the household was able to sleep, but once Mary knew what was expected of her, she drew on an inner strength she could count on. She'd called on it many times before.

Mary could barely see Russ now in the morning dimness as he moved among the various outbuildings, his movements steady and consistent. Her husband would feed chickens and pigs, tend to the horses and calves, milk their two cows, all before breakfast. She had already pumped and carried in water, started the fire, lit lamps, made coffee. She left the kitchen to awaken Rita and Ellen and then returned to stir the oatmeal.

"You always get up this early?" Danny McCool startled her as he walked into the kitchen.

"Always." She turned briefly to nod at Mr. McCool, reaching to her neck to make sure her robe was fully buttoned.

"Smells good. You always eat like this?"

"Every day. Have a seat, Mr. McCool. Russell will be in soon."

"Call me Danny. Please."

The girls rambled into the kitchen, greeted their guest, and went straight into their daily routine. Ellen pulled on black boots, grabbed a sweater, and went outside to feed the dogs. Rita cut slices of bread for their school lunches.

When Russell and Ellen returned through the back door, Mary scraped the scrambled eggs into a bowl and declared that breakfast was ready. Rita placed the pan of oatmeal on the table next to a canning jar stuffed with orange bittersweet that served as a bit of decoration. After everyone was seated, Russell prayed.

Mary lifted the bowl toward their guest, determined to be cordial. "So, where do you folks call home?"

"The wonderful city of Chicago," Danny said, piling eggs onto his plate.

"Chicago?" Ellen stared at him. "What's it like there? We've never been to Chicago."

"Now, let the man eat, Ellen," Russell said.

"It's all right," Danny said. "I don't mind." He turned to Ellen. "Chicago is a grand city, all hustle and bustle, wonderful things going on there. It has its problems, of course, but I wish you could see the Merchandize Mart. I was just there last week. Biggest building in the world."

"I'd love to go to Chicago," Ellen said. "Do you fly your airplane a lot?" "Speaking of flying," interrupted Russell. "Let's talk about your plane. I'm going to call Bud Devore today. Runs a gas station in Rensselaer and worked on planes in the war. Thought he could help you out."

"I can check the engine myself," said Danny, as casually as if he were talking about buying some shoes.

"If I were you, I'd be wanting some help on that," Russell said. "You may not be so lucky next time." He frowned over his coffee cup.

"You're right. There is the wing and landing gear I may need help on, too."

"I'm sure with Bud's help we can get her fixed. We know how to make do around here. That's how we all keep afloat."

"Of course," said Danny. "Hard times everywhere, I'm sure. I've been fortunate, myself. But, Jean, well, I'd have to say Jean has been somewhat spoiled." He looked toward the sitting room, where Jean was still fast asleep. "She could not survive this hearty life out here in the country, no electricity and all. I love her dearly, but it's probably best she go home today. We'll get the old plane up and running, keep the old man happy. Of course I'll pay you folks for your trouble."

"We'll see how it goes," Russell said.

Danny winked at Ellen. "More card tricks today, girls?"

"Can we stay home from school?" Ellen asked, turning toward her mother.

"Certainly not," said Mary. "Finish up and get ready. The hack will be here soon."

The girls carried their dishes to the sink and left the room.

"So, just what do you do in Chicago?" Russell asked. "If you don't mind me asking."

"Several things, actually. I work for Jean's father. That's his airplane out there in your field. I give airplane rides at fairs. I went to flight school at Terre Haute here in Indiana, and I did, in fact, meet Amelia

Earhart at Purdue University. Shook hands with her after her lecture. So, that's me in a nutshell, so to speak." He reached for the bowl of applesauce. "You are the best cook I have ever met, Mary Walstra."

Mary blushed as she picked up each dirty plate and placed them in a stack.

By Monday afternoon, the party line buzzed with news. Cars flowed past the Walstra house in an irregular stream hoping to see the plane. Some folks stopped, interrupting Russell's work, asking to see the airplane up close. Russell walked back to the field with Brady from the *Rensselaer Republican*. Brady took several photographs of the Fairfield 24 airplane, which looked like a toy out of place among the cornstalks, one wing up and one bent sideways on the ground. Danny McCool posed by its side, elbow on a wing, one foot on the cockeyed landing gear. *Like he thinks he's someone famous*, thought Russell.

"We'll have the story in next Monday's paper," Brady announced.

Russell and Danny walked around the plane several times with Brady trailing behind, but the only real damage seemed to be to the landing gear and wing—and the engine, of course. Danny poked around the cockpit and then climbed out carrying a small suitcase, a woman's purple hat, and a shaving kit.

Brady quizzed Danny, "What was the problem that you ended up out here?"

"Clearly engine trouble," Danny McCool said, smiling and waving at the few people milling around. "But this was a good place to land, the ground being so hard and dry before it rained. I had to go around that storm, which was part of the problem. You can't fly through a thunderstorm. I was headed back to Chicago and it was getting late, then the engine trouble. So there you go. I'm staying here with the Walstra family until I can get her fixed up. Wonderful people."

"No injuries to yourself or your passenger?" Brady asked, taking notes on a small pad of paper.

"All shipshape. Just a little banged and bruised. Miss Swanson will be returning to Chicago today."

Just before suppertime, Jean's father arrived in a cream-colored Ford Roadster, dressed like a banker in a gray suit and hat. He didn't stay long. Despite his small size, he stood up straight before Danny McCool, speaking directly and to the point.

"I can't believe the chances you take…and with my daughter." He punched two fingers against Danny's chest. "Don't come back to Chicago until my plane is restored to its original condition, and we'll talk about your employment then. My daughter says you were doing tricks in that plane."

"No tricks, sir, just a little wing dip here and there." He didn't appear to be intimidated at all.

"You should have been back on Saturday."

"I'm sorry, sir. I told you, we had engine trouble. But as you can see, we're fine and the plane can be fixed."

Mr. Swanson turned from Danny, shaking his head. He escorted Jean, who looked refreshed and regal in a purple hat with soaring feather, to the waiting car. Russell and his family assembled around them. Jean thanked the Walstras but had nothing to say to Danny.

Mr. Swanson rolled down his window and handed Danny an envelope. "Here's your pay from last month. There's a little extra for fuel, but I'm not paying for any repairs. You'll take it out of your pay."

He started the car and drove away without a look back.

The Walstras and Danny stood in a group, watching the car until it was out of sight.

"Well, that's that," said Danny McCool, slapping his hands together as if nothing unusual had happened. "What are we having for supper here on the farm?"

Mary took the girls' hands and walked toward the house. Russell stepped toward Danny. "We've got work to do in the barn before supper. As long as you're here, you'll have to do your share." Russell Walstra was a practical man.

Danny glanced down at his white shoes. "I'll need different shoes and clothes, of course."

Russell walked away without comment, and Danny followed. In the kitchen Russell eyed Danny from head to foot.

"I reckon we're about the same size, only you're taller and your feet are bigger." Russell went upstairs to the bedroom and returned with denim work pants and a brown shirt. "Try my four-buckle over-boots with these wool socks until I can see if one of my brothers has something that'll work."

Danny pulled on the too-short pants and too-small boots, then followed Russell to the barn, where two cows stood waiting behind a gate.

"I noticed that basketball rim you have on the side of the barn," said Danny. "Do you play basketball?"

"Did when I was a kid."

"Do you have a basketball?"

"Not with air in it." Russell patted the cow's nose and opened the gate. He scooped feed into the trough and turned over a wooden box for Danny to sit on next to the cow's flank. After a short lesson, Danny sent spurts of milk pinging into the bucket.

"I was actually born here in Indiana, in Indianapolis," Danny said. Russell nodded but kept moving, setting a bucket under the other cow and lowering himself onto a three-legged stool. "My father did pretty well in business, at the glove factory there. Then he moved on to other business. I was lucky enough to get a scholarship and go to college. First one in the family." Milk accumulated slowly in the buckets.

"How about you, Russ?"

"Grew up north of here, in Demotte. Mostly Dutch families," Russell said.

"Ah, the Dutch."

"Grandpa Casper Walstra came from Holland. Two brothers and I moved down this way. Had a little disagreement with Father, but he's passed on now. Mother and sister and two other brothers still live in Demotte."

"Family. Don't see my family much, since I've been in Chicago," Danny said.

Russell finished with his cow and moved over to check on Danny.

"Here, let me finish up. Ain't got all day." Danny stood and Russell sat down on the box.

"How do you manage all this yourself?" Danny asked.

"We brothers work together on the crops. They live down the way at the other end of the farm, see." He nodded toward the west. "Helps since I don't have any sons, at least none living." He finished the milking and stood up as tall as he could, looking down to Danny, who sat on a sack of feed near the wall.

"We do all right, as good as anybody around here. Plan to get a tractor next year, God willing, between the three of us." He looked through the side door of the barn and pointed. "Working on building up our herd, if you want to call it that. We've got four calves now. Takes time. And there's so much we got no control over."

That was enough talking for Russell. He led the cows back outside, showed Danny how to strain the milk, and directed him to carry the milk can to the milk house, where they placed it in cool water.

The sky was getting dark. The men walked toward the house, where a faint gleam of light shone from the kitchen window and the smell of baked corn bread invited them inside. They watched Mary place a pot of great northern beans on the table and fork a chunk of ham the size of a small cantaloupe onto a plate. She used the wooden spoon to scrape the meat off the bone and then placed it back in the pot. A plate of sliced tomatoes and onions sat next to a mound of corn bread cut in cubes, each the size of half a brick.

"My favorite meal," said Russell, winking at Mary, who now stood by the stove rubbing butter on her hands.

Russell noticed Danny watching his wife. "The butter helps keep her skin soft," he said.

Danny raised his index finger. "You know, I've got some lotion that belonged to Jean. Found it in my bag." He retreated to the front porch and returned with a bottle of Chamberlain's hand lotion. He handed it to Mary. She turned it over in her hand as if it were precious jewelry.

She looked up to him. "Thank you, but you say this is Jean's?"

"She can get more," he said, waving his hand in the air as if to brush away any concerns she might have.

Mary dished out the ham and beans and handed the plates around the table.

"I must say, it's been a good day," said Danny. "Except, of course, for Jean. I doubt we'll get married now."

Russell reached for the plate of tomatoes, unsure what to say. The family ate in silence to the sounds of scraping silverware and the clink of dishes. He had told Ellen not to speak up so much and she obeyed.

"I wanted us to elope," Danny said after several minutes. "I took Jean to Terre Haute, showed her around the college, thought everything was just right. But when I told her we could get married in Indianapolis that very night, she wanted nothing to do with it." Danny took a drink of milk. He shrugged his shoulders.

"Then we had to get around that storm, had to land, and now I'm here with you all." He swung his fork in a semicircle, taking them all in, and then jabbed it into another square of corn bread.

"Maybe she just needs time to cool off," Mary said. "Once you get the plane fixed—"

Russell broke in, "We'll talk to Devore, see what we need to get that landing gear fixed. Check the engine."

"Sounds like a good idea." He cut his corn bread in half. "Say, is there a reason you don't use your radio?" Danny asked. "I saw your Philco in there by the davenport." He nodded toward the sitting room.

"Battery's dead. I'll get us a new one, directly," said Russell.

Mary walked to the upright cupboard and took down a milk pitcher with a blue windmill design on its side. She scattered coins onto the table.

"Probably need a little more egg money before we'll have enough," she said.

"I'll get you one," Danny said. "How'd that be?" He slapped his hand down on the table. "We can't do without the radio, can we, girls?" Ellen smiled, showing all her teeth, and Rita giggled.

Mary placed the pitcher back on the shelf.

Does this man have an endless supply of money? Russell wondered.

CHAPTER 4

Summer 1968

I T WAS IN JULY OF 1968 THAT I FIRST LEARNED ABOUT DANIEL MCCOOL. I spent a lot of time that summer with Grandma Walstra on the old farm about two miles northwest of Remington where Mom and Aunt Rita grew up. When Grandpa Walstra died, he left Grandma with a well-kept farm that was all paid off. It hadn't changed much over the years, except they had modernized the kitchen and put in bathrooms. Dad built a garage next to the house, but some of the small outbuildings had been torn down and replaced with flower gardens. Grandma was determined to stay on the farm, so she rented out their forty acres for others to plant in corn and soybeans. She was lonely, though, especially after Mom died. I think she found ways for me to help her, just to keep her company and also so she could give me some spending money, as she liked to call it.

This particular day Grandma Walstra and I sat on the floor of her upstairs bedroom, boxes stacked around us in pyramids. We were sorting through papers and old books and photos. She said she was going to get organized. It looked to me, as we pulled items out of boxes and threw very little away, that we were not making any headway. After sifting through a pile of old photographs, I lifted up a black-and-white photo of a handsome man in a leather bomber jacket with a young woman at his side. It wasn't any of our relatives that I knew of.

"Who's this, Grandma?"

She took the photo from me. "That's Danny McCool and his fiancée, Jean. He's the aviator who landed in the field behind our house back in 1938."

"What aviator?" I asked.

"Didn't I tell you that story?"

"No." I scooted closer and turned down the radio. Sounded like an adventure to me.

"Well, it was a beautiful fall evening, not hot and miserable like today," she said, fanning herself with the photograph. I noticed bits of dust swirl in the sunbeam that fell between us. "The sun was just going down beyond the cornfield there past the barn and a storm was coming in from the south."

I looked out the window at the corn standing in shiny green rows in the sunlight. I pictured how it would look in the fall, cornstalks dry and crackly, during one of those still moments in the evening when the air looks golden and long shadows slant across the fields.

She continued, "I was washing dishes with your mom and Aunt Rita. Grandpa was in the living room drinking coffee. And Danny McCool just landed his little airplane in our cornfield." She handed the photograph back to me.

"So that's why you have their picture?"

"Yes, this particular one was taken right after he returned to Chicago, before he and Jean decided to go their separate ways. 'So you'll remember this crazy aviator,' he wrote."

Grandma shuffled through the box, a smile on her face. "He sends us a picture or card every Christmas, always with a friendly little note about the weather in Houston, where he lived for a while, or about his grandchildren. He was grateful to us. He stayed with us for over a week until the plane was fixed. A problem with the fuel line or the engine or something. We didn't have motels at every country crossroad back then where people could stay."

"So you weren't afraid of them? They could have been criminals."

Grandma laughed. "No… No." She stared at the picture. "You watch too much TV. They were nice people. Mr. McCool was a pilot in World War II. Oh, here's another one." She handed me a photo of the same man in a military uniform, standing by a fighter plane.

"He's kinda good-looking."

"He certainly was. He ended up marrying someone else, not Jean. I think there's a picture of them in here somewhere after they were married."

"So, he was a war pilot, a war hero?"

"I suppose he could have been a hero. He never spoke of the war, soldiers never do, but this picture taken by his plane was sent from England."

She paused again, staring at the curling photograph. She moved to get up. "Well, I think we need to go fix supper. I've been sitting here on the floor too long."

I stood and pulled at her elbow to help her stand up.

"It's the arthritis. How about some fried chicken, kiddo?"

We were just finishing supper when we heard a horn outside.

"There's your dad," Grandma said. "He won't want to wait."

I rolled the rest of my chicken leg in a napkin, wiped my hands on a towel, and opened the kitchen door.

"'Bye, Grandma." I let the screen door slam shut behind me.

I slid into the front seat with Dad. "Why didn't you or Mom tell me about Daniel McCool, who landed the plane here?"

"Him? I don't know, seemed like a slick guy from Chicago, seemed out of place here. I remember his little plane, though. A Fairchild. I was just eighteen and got to help work on it with Bud Devore."

As we reached the edge of Remington, the sunset that looked like orange and pink watercolors quickly turned to gray.

Dad went to the living room and turned on the TV while I sat down at the kitchen table, reaching behind me to the bookshelf that sagged under the weight of the entire set of *World Book Encyclopedias*. I looked up airplanes. I was fascinated to read about the small fighter planes that Mr. McCool must have flown during the war. Those pilots were true heroes. Most of them never came back, I learned.

I carried an encyclopedia into the living room to show Dad, but he was asleep in his chair in front of the TV. I laid the book down, sat on the couch, and watched Lawrence Welk, who matched his orchestra tonight in a suit the color of orange Popsicles.

When I wasn't at Grandma Walstra's during the weekdays that summer, I was at Aunt Rita's. Lana and I explored the woods. We drew pictures of the neighbor's horses. We swam in the creek and caught crawdads with her twin brothers, little Ned and Ted.

"If only we had our own horses that we could ride," Lana said.

We had to be content with just looking at the ones that sometimes came close enough to the fence that we could pet their noses, but at least that was something.

I decided one day that we should play Robinson Crusoe. Like I said, my imagination had come back. I was familiar with the story of Robinson Crusoe and told Lana we needed to build a shelter. I used my knife to cut long, leafy branches, which we leaned against a big oak tree. Since we were pretending to be shipwrecked, we were able to salvage supplies from the boat, like Robinson Crusoe did, which in our case were hot dogs, peanut butter, and crackers. We also salvaged a seaman's trunk, actually a small cardboard box, a knife, a spyglass (we substituted Uncle Phil's telescope), matches, and a fishing pole. We tried to catch fish in the creek, which didn't work, but we did make a fire and roasted our hot dogs. By afternoon we were sweating even in the shade of our shelter.

"Let's go check out the people in the church," I said.

"We could pretend they're the native islanders," Lana suggested, since she knew I liked to stay in character.

I turned the telescope toward the church. "The natives are home. They're outside hanging up some laundry."

"Do those people even have a washing machine or bathrooms?"

"I don't know."

We left our camp and walked up to the house, where little black bugs pressed against the screen door. Aunt Rita stood at the sink squeezing a purple cheesecloth-covered ball of raspberry pulp. Dark juice dripped into a bowl.

"Isn't the jelly a wonderful color in the sunlight?" Rita said. The eight jars lined up on the counter filtered the light like stained-glass windows.

"It's pretty, Mom," Lana said. "We're going to ride our bikes down by the church."

Aunt Rita looked through the door to our mess outside and then to Lana.

"We'll clean all that up when we get back," she said.

Aunt Rita must have been satisfied with the answer. "I've been thinking about those people down the road," she said. "They're probably melting in there. Why don't you take them one of our fans." She pointed her stained hand toward the round fan oscillating in front of the window. "There's an extra one like that in the closet."

We walked through the living room to the closet. Aunt Rita had the kind of house you'd see in *Better Homes & Gardens*. Her own oil paintings hung on the walls, and the furniture was unique, an antique rolltop desk, a lamp stand with ball and claw legs. Every piece of furniture and every item on her shelves had a story behind it.

"This green bowl belonged to Mrs. Landon, the jeweler's mother," she liked to explain. "This little shelf is from the old drugstore at Wolcott." Stories like that. I liked the pitcher with the blue windmill on its side. It had belonged to Grandma Walstra and came from what she referred to as the Old Country, straight from Holland.

We found the fan and put it in the basket on the front of Lana's bike, then drove down to the church. This time the girl our age answered the door.

"Hi," I said. "It's us again. My name is Jude, and this is my cousin Lana. We thought you might be able to use a fan." I pointed back to the house and said, "Lana lives down in that blue house and I live in Remington."

"I'm Lydia. Are those y'all's horses across the road?" She had a Kentucky accent that I liked instantly.

Lana said, "No, I wish they were. I love horses."

"Me, too." She turned around and called, "Mom, come here."

She had opened the door wide. I saw her mom at the back of the room standing by a hot plate with a wooden spoon. The amber church windows had been pushed open for air, but I didn't see a fan anywhere.

Her mom came to the door, pushing her hair back under a pink bandana.

"It's just an extra fan. We don't need it," Lana offered.

"My name is Caroline Mayhugh." She offered a weary smile, her shoulders more relaxed this time. "And thank you. We don't need any help, but if this fan is extra, I expect we could use it." She was holding the baby and nodded toward the floor. "You can set it down there."

I stepped inside the door and placed the fan on the floor, giving me enough time to quickly scan the room. The church pews were arranged liked movable walls to divide the single room into living areas. Blankets rolled up in bundles lay on the pews next to stacks of clothes and boxes. At the back of the room, two metal tables stood end to end like a kitchen counter holding the hot plate, dishes, cereal boxes, and a large tub. The only other appliance I saw was a small refrigerator.

"Thank your mother for me," Mrs. Mayhugh said. I turned and stepped back outside. She had a mild accent, not as strong as Lydia's.

As we rode our bikes back down the road, Lana said, "How can they live in there? How do they take a bath or wash their dishes? Did you see a bathroom?"

"I don't know. They're kind of like Robinson Crusoe living there, surviving on what they have, improvising. The house didn't seem dirty, though. I mean, there were some toys on the floor, but everything else seemed organized. I like the way they talk."

We pedaled back to Lana's house, where Uncle Phil was just getting out of his car.

"Hi, Dad," Lana called out as we parked our bikes.

Uncle Phil raised his briefcase in a salute to us, revealing underarm dampness on his white shirt.

"Mom made jelly," she said.

"I hope she's got some iced tea. Boy oh boy, is it hot." He turned to me. "How's the stargazing Jude?"

"Okay. I've noticed Mars lately."

It was one thing we could always talk about. A couple of times he had gotten his telescope out and he'd shown me the rings around Saturn and some star clusters.

"I see you've got the scope out," he said. "Not too many stars out right now, huh."

The telescope stood under the trees in the yard where we'd left it.

"Sorry, Uncle Phil. You said I could borrow it, though. Right?"

"Sure. I hardly have time to use it anymore. More important things to do now." He held up his suitcase representing his job and pointed his left arm toward the twins, who were playing in the sandbox.

"What were you looking at in broad daylight, anyway?" he asked.

"Nothing. We were playing Robinson Crusoe. It was our spyglass."

Uncle Phil was not Lana's real dad. I always thought he seemed a little out of place, an insurance salesman in suit and tie with crew-cut hair living out here in the country. When Uncle Phil was with adults, he talked about boring statistics, insurance stuff. Dad explained it to me by saying, "Opposites attract." That's the only reason Phil could have ended up with Aunt Rita, because there is nothing artistic or musical about Uncle Phil.

Mom told me that Rita married him out of desperation. As soon as she said it, she added, "But I shouldn't have told you that. Just forget it." But you can't forget things like that.

Mom explained it all to me one day while we were picking green beans in the garden. She said Rita married a guy named Curtis right after she graduated from high school. He was a "musician," she added, making quote marks in the air with green beans and rolling her eyes. They got married and moved to Dayton because Curtis got a job at Goodyear Tire. But since he wanted to be a "musician," again the quote marks in the air, he ended up quitting his job.

"Was he a good musician?"

"I don't know, but that's no way to make money. So Rita had to work and then she had Lana. Finally they got a divorce."

She broke the green beans in half and tossed them into the basket.

"Rita had no choice. She came back to live with Grandma and Grandpa until she met Phil. Phil was just the first guy that came along," she said. She shrugged her shoulders. "But it's turned out all right and now they have the twins. They're so cute even though they look like Phil." That made us both laugh.

I missed Mom's detailed explanations and heart-to-heart talks. She talked to me so much more than Dad did.

It wasn't long before we saw the girls from the church again. Lana and I were walking down the path by the railroad tracks heading west from town when we saw Deborah and Lydia walking toward us on the tracks themselves.

"Hey," Lydia said.

"Did you walk all the way from your house?"

"Sure, it's only about three miles. We walked everywhere in Kentucky. Up and down hills, too."

I looked at their legs, calves rounded out with muscle.

"Where y'all going?" Lydia asked.

"To a farm pond not far from here. Dad knows the farmer and he doesn't care if we go there. You can come along if you want."

They changed direction and continued with us toward the pond.

"Come up here on the tracks," Lydia said.

"Dad likes us to stay on the path," I said. "A train might come along."

Lydia looked at her sister and laughed. "You could see a train a hundred miles off."

I looked down the tracks in both directions. "Yeah, I guess you'd have to be blind and deaf not to know a train was coming." I started up the short rise to the tracks. Lana must have agreed with me because she followed.

Stepping on each railroad tie made our steps too short, but reaching every other tie was too long. We balanced on the rails, seeing how far we could go without falling off. Before long we were laughing together and running across the field toward the pond.

Lana and I had brought our fishing poles. Deborah sat down by us on the grass and watched as I opened up Dad's tackle box. I heard splashing and looked up to see Lydia sloshing into the water in her underpants.

Lana giggled.

"Y'all coming in?" Lydia called to us.

I'd never stripped down to underwear out in the open.

Deborah said, "Y'all go on. I don't want to." She never seemed to be in a good mood.

Lana said, "I think I'll just stay here and fish." She pulled the fishing line to straighten it out.

"Come on, don't be chicken," Lydia called.

I took off my shoes and socks, then finally my shorts, stood up in underpants and tank top, and walked out into the water. It was a hot day and the cool water felt good. I felt like I was breaking rules, no bathing suit, no adult supervision, and it felt good. Once I got used to the cold, I held my nose and went under the water. We splashed around awhile and then went up to the bank. I needed time to dry out before I went back home. Deborah was using my fishing pole.

Lydia sat down on a grassy spot in the sand. "We fished a lot in Kentucky," she said. "Got blue gill and catfish. Ate fish all the time."

"Why'd you move here?"

Deborah said, "We just wanted to move here, that's all." She had become sarcastic all of a sudden. "Why do y'all live here yourselves?"

"Just always have. I'd go somewhere else if I could."

Lydia said, "I like it here. It's a lot better than where we used to live."

I wondered what could be worse than living in a one-room church.

Deborah glared at Lydia, as if to tell her to shut up.

"It sure as heck was no fun living with Dad, Deborah."

"You don't need to tell no one our business, Lydia."

Lana and I sat silent.

"Hey, we all got problems," I offered.

Deborah looked at me. "You don't have problems."

I thought about this as Lana and I walked alone back to town, hoping the sun would dry our clothes before we reached home. We did have problems. It bothered me when my dad didn't have enough work to keep him busy. I'd go by the kitchen sometimes and see him sitting at the table drinking coffee, leaning over the paper or just gazing out the window. Once I stared at his back while he sat there. He was wearing a white T-shirt and he just looked smaller than usual. With Mom gone, he would often sit with the radio on, listening to some country station I wasn't familiar with. I felt sorry for him and I hated that feeling.

The first time I'd felt that sorry feeling was the winter before Mom died. We were bringing Marty home from the hospital where he'd gone for pneumonia, and we stopped at some little restaurant in Lafayette. It was gray November, we were tired, everything seemed sad. I looked at our waitress in her tan dress and red apron. Her name was Barb according to her name tag and I felt sorry for her. She was doing her job, being cheerful, and I wondered what her life was like. She was old, maybe thirty-five, and I thought, *Is this her whole life?* But to see Dad like that, that was the worst kind of sorry.

Lana had been lagging behind but caught up with me.

"Your clothes dry yet?" she asked.

"Getting there." I snapped back to the present. "That was fun swimming in the pond like that. I like Lydia. I like that she's not afraid to do things."

"I didn't want to get in that dirty water, plus you know we aren't supposed to swim in that pond, and definitely not in just our underwear," Lana said.

You'll never do anything exciting then, I thought to myself.

CHAPTER 5

October 1938
Tuesday

FARM WORK DOESN'T STOP JUST BECAUSE THERE'S A GUEST IN THE HOUSE and a plane to fix. The corn was dry-crisp in the field, the sky vivid blue like Delft pottery. It was time to start picking. Russ harnessed the two horses after morning chores and drove off in the wagon to join his brothers in the field. He would be there all day except for a dinner break at noon, when hopefully Devore would come as promised to look at the plane. If all went well, a couple loads of corn would go in the crib today. Mary and the girls would do the evening chores on days like this.

Russell put Danny to work. He helped with the morning chores, gathered eggs and fed chickens with the girls, cleaned lamp chimneys, and picked apples. When Russell came in at noon, he found Danny sitting on the front step by a basket of apples, leaning forward with his elbows on his knees. He could tell the aviator wasn't used to hard work. Russell handed him a tin cup of water, and together they stared across the field to where the wingtip of the plane jutted above the corn.

Devore arrived shortly after noon in a dark blue truck with his young apprentice, Robert James. Russell and Danny joined them at the plane with cups of coffee in hand. Danny seemed somewhat revived after eating a plate of warmed-up beans. They jacked the plane up and leveled it by placing bricks under the struts. It looked like the left wing, though badly bent, could be fixed. The struts would also need some work. Devore then turned to the engine. He opened the compartment and called Robert over to look.

"Now, this is the difference between a car and a plane," he instructed, speaking in great detail of combustion and cylinders and carburetors. Danny added a few comments of his own. Devore poked around for a while before turning back to Danny and Russell. "Everything looks pretty good to me. This is the first time I've worked on a Fairchild, but it looks okay."

"I did tinker with it yesterday," said Danny. "Added some oil, cleaned things up a bit."

"Seems to be out of fuel," Devore said.

"I'll be needing fuel, of course."

"Probably have to get it from the airport in Lafayette. You able to pay for it?"

"Yes."

Devore removed the plane's tires and handed them to Robert. "Take these on up to my truck so we can get them some air and check for leaks." Robert put one tire under each arm and walked toward the house.

Danny handed Devore a twenty-dollar bill. "That should take care of the fuel and your help."

Devore wiped the grease from his hand and stuck the bill in his pocket. He squinted up at Danny. "Did you just run out fuel? Was that the problem?"

"Well, my fuel gauge has been acting up, but I believe there was more to it than that."

Devore looked to Russell and jerked a thumb toward Danny. "I think your man just ran out of gas."

Danny continued, "...and then there was the storm." Devore shook his head and walked away.

CHAPTER 6

Summer 1968

G RANDMA WALSTRA WASN'T FINISHED SORTING THINGS IN HER bedroom, so a few days later we were back at it again. She had emptied some boxes out of the closet, and now an odd assortment of items such as shoes, empty perfume bottles, and broken toys was lined up on the floor next to shoe boxes full of papers. I told her I didn't think we were getting anything organized, just making it worse, but she said, "This is good for us." She walked over to her bed and sat down next to a black oblong case. "And you won't believe what I found."

She flipped up two metal clasps along the side of the case and lifted the lid on its hinges to reveal a black clarinet in three pieces, each nested in a purple velvet compartment.

"What is it?" I asked.

"It's your mother's clarinet." She rubbed her hand over the shiny keys. "I want you to have it. It belonged to my father, who played in an orchestra. He handed it down to me, and I passed it on to your mother. She played wonderfully."

I picked up the largest clarinet piece and pushed down the tabs. I felt the smooth velvet lining of the case.

"The music teacher took a special interest in her even when she was young, took her under his wing. She was in the little orchestra they had in high school and could play along with songs on the radio. Like Benny Goodman."

She twisted the three clarinet parts together and held it up in front of her. "Of course, you'll need new reeds. This one is worn out and split."

I lifted the clarinet to my lips and blew into the mouthpiece, but only a loud squawk came out. It smelled and tasted musty.

"It'll take some practice," Grandma said.

"I could play this in Band next year. It will remind me of Mom."

"Well, that was my idea." She smiled.

I put the clarinet back in the case, clasped it shut, and laid it on the floor close to me.

We started in on the row of items before us, examining them piece by piece, placing some things in the trash, others in a box to stow away again. We threw away old receipts and magazines. Then Grandma produced another box of photos. She handed me a heavy brown photo, a family portrait. She pointed out herself, a little girl with black hair hanging in waves over her short white dress, standing in front of her parents, Henry and Leah Fontaine. Two older brothers stood on one side and an older sister on the other. Each person looked gravely serious except Grandma, who had a slight smile that showed her dimples.

"You were such a cute little girl," I said. "Why isn't anyone else smiling?"

"That's the way they took formal pictures back then."

She showed me another thick, brownish photo of her as a young lady. Her dark hair was piled on top of her head. She wore a blouse buttoned all the way up to her neck. She had a slight smile in this one also, one corner of her mouth turned up and dimples clearly visible.

"Can you tell that's me? I've changed a little since then." She laughed. She reached up and patted her white hair. Only a few strands of black could still be seen.

"You look like Mom in this one."

"Yes, we do favor. She had my hair and eyes."

I stared at the likeness while she shuffled through the box. She handed me a photo of my dad as a young man standing on the front porch, arms folded and head tossed back.

"This was taken when he was visiting the farm, courting your mom. You can take this home with you," she said.

"Why aren't we close to Dad's family, the Jameses, like we are to you?"

"Families are different. Some aren't as close-knit. The Jameses…I don't know. I guess they moved to Tennessee because they like the weather down there, and the bank offered him that job, but I don't see how anyone could move so far away from family."

"They're getting old. Grandpa James told Dad he was getting too old for Indiana winters."

Grandma said, "Ha, they're no older than I am, and that was three or four years ago when they moved." She put the lid back on the box. "Your grandma James probably made the final decision. Grandpa James does whatever she wants. Sorry, I just think she can be a little bossy. I still think of how she barged in after your mom died, but then the rest of us were in such a state maybe we needed her to do our thinking for us. Don't think ill of her, Judy. I'm just rambling on."

"They want us to move to Tennessee, but Dad said he's staying put."

"Well, good for him. After losing Ellen, I wouldn't want to lose you, too."

The Jameses stayed with us for a whole week after Mom died. The very day after the funeral, they took Dad into the bedroom and all over the house to go through Mom's things. Aunt Rita and Grandma were there, too. Grandma James convinced everyone that it was the right thing to do. She was authoritative. She took charge, bustling about, skirt swishing, bracelets jingling. The rest of us were still in shock. I thought they were going to throw away everything, like Mom never existed, but it wasn't that way at all. They kept all sorts of things to remember her by, pictures, fancy earrings, chunky necklaces, an old china doll, books. Her vanity stayed in the bedroom filled with these keepsakes, much of it set aside to be passed on to me. But clothing, cosmetics, things like that, were thrown or given away.

The Jameses were with us all week, sitting around the kitchen table talking to Dad, waking me up for school, heating up the food people brought us. When the week was over, they went back to Tennessee.

Grandma Walstra picked up a cigar box from her dresser before we went downstairs. "You take these home, too. They're pictures of your mom. I think you should have them."

I opened the box. The square photo on top revealed my young mother, dark hair in waves, sitting on the hood of an old car. I shut the lid. I'd save this treasure for later. I picked up the clarinet case and we went downstairs.

Back home I went into my room, shut the door, opened the cigar box, and looked at each picture carefully. Tears came to my eyes but I kept going. I laid all the curling photos gently back into the cigar box and put them in my top dresser drawer next to a small box of Mom's jewelry. I took the photo of Mom sitting on the car and put it in the corner of the frame that held the formal wedding picture of Mom and Dad. It sat on the table by my bed. I put the clarinet case on the shelf in my closet and went to the mirror to see if my eyes still looked red.

I heard Dad call, "Jude, come downstairs. Gonna have a good supper tonight."

I was starving. When I got to the bottom of the stairs, I saw Aunt Rita uncovering a casserole dish on the kitchen table.

"I had some extra chicken so I fixed you some chicken and noodles," she said. "I've also got some applesauce from last fall."

Dad set a carton of milk on the counter while Marty scooped out a mound of food that filled half of his plate.

"Wait for me," I said. I grabbed a plate, spooned out a normal serving, and sat down by Marty.

"You staying, Rita?" Dad asked.

"Oh, no," she said. "We already ate." She pointed out the window. "Phil brought the telescope down for Judy."

My mouth was too full to speak, but I looked wide-eyed at Aunt Rita and then turned to the back door window where I could see Uncle Phil carrying the telescope under his arm, tripod legs sticking out behind him. He set it up at one side of the yard, looked up at the sky, and then moved it to the middle of the yard. I could tell he was looking for a spot without tree limbs and streetlights. The shed door was open, so I knew Lana was in there with the twins looking for Marty's old rusty Tonka trucks to play with like usual.

Rita asked Dad how his work was coming along while I quickly ate and then joined Uncle Phil outside.

He was squinting into the little viewfinder that sat on top of the main telescope.

"Look here, Jude. You'll always want to have this fine-tuned before you do some stargazing. Just adjust these little screws and sight it in on some object like the top of that light pole. I've tried several places in your yard, none ideal of course since we're in town, but you can get a few glimpses of the sky." He handed me a small box. "Here are some extra eyepieces, different magnifications, and this little pocket guide to the constellations should help you."

"Thanks, Uncle Phil." I sat down on the ground and flipped through the pages.

It turned out they didn't leave right away. Uncle Phil wanted to wait until after dark so we could look at the moon together through the telescope. Rita cleaned the kitchen and cooked some pudding for us all, which she carried outside on a tray with some instant iced tea. The adults mumbled quietly in the background while Lana and I played with the twins. We used the Tonka trucks to build roads and gathered up twigs to build small fences. Sometimes I could overhear the adults. The conversation circled around several times to how we were doing and how Dad's work was going, but I could also hear Phil's loud laugh and knew Dad was telling some of his jokes. It made me feel good. I loved it when Dad made people laugh. I liked having Rita around, too. She reminded me of Mom, and made me miss her, but she also somehow seemed to fill in for her. I looked at everyone around me on this warm summer night. It was like happiness and sadness mixed together at the same time.

As the sky got dark, the moon was clearly visible in the space between the trees. Uncle Phil noticed it, too, and joined me at the telescope. Everyone else went inside and Dad turned off the backyard light. The moon looked like a pie cut in half.

"This is good," Phil said. "When the moon is full you can't see anything, it's too bright and all the features are washed out, but we'll be able to see mountains and craters along the edge there." He adjusted the telescope, and we took turns looking at the sharp edges of the moon.

"Uncle Phil, does the moon ever make you feel sad or happy or even…what's the right word…nostalgic?"

Tonight the moon made me feel good. It just looked like half a cream pie or an orange wedge. Other times it looked scary or caused a sad longing inside me.

Phil stood up straight after bending over the eyepiece and put his hands on his hips.

"Well, it's just a big, cold rock, actually. It does exert a pull on the ocean tides, but I'm not sure about its effect on people. It doesn't even give off any light by itself, it just reflects the sun."

"Yeah, I know."

"And we always see the same side, we only see the bright side of the moon. We never see the other side, the dark side. We have no idea what's back there. There could be an entire city of aliens."

I jerked my head around to Uncle Phil and saw his face barely illuminated by the moonlight, staring up into the sky.

"Do you really think so?"

"Who knows? There could be strange creatures up there getting ready to come visit our planet, they could be talking about the strange people on Earth."

"Really?"

"Ah, no. Just kidding. There's nothing up there."

I was surprised by Uncle Phil, he didn't usually joke around. We laughed together, and then I squinted into the eyepiece one last time. The moon was passing out of the field of view.

"But do you think the moon can affect us?" I asked. I was thinking of the werewolf movies, even though I knew they weren't true.

Uncle Phil thought a second. "Well, there's the word *moonstruck*. I would say it's just a superstition that the moon, especially a full moon, can cause people to go mad or even fall in love."

"So maybe it does affect people."

Uncle Phil scratched the back of his neck. "You might want to ask your aunt Rita about these things, but maybe the moon just reflects what we're feeling already, just like it reflects the sun."

"Maybe."

"Oh, I get it." Uncle Phil laughed and then whispered like it was a big secret, "Do you have a boyfriend? Have you fallen in love?"

I felt my face turn red in the dark. "No, not really. I wish I did."

Rita turned on the light at the back door and spoke into the darkness. "Phil, I think it's time to get the twins home. They're getting rambunctious."

Uncle Phil lifted the telescope and collapsed its legs. He handed it to me.

"It's all yours now." We walked toward the house.

"And don't rush the boyfriend business. You're way too young for that. You've got plenty of time."

The next week Lana and I stood at the front door of the old church.

"Lydia's out in back there somewhere," Caroline said.

Lana and I walked around to the back of the church calling out, "Lyd, where are you?" We didn't see her in the barren brown space with a few tufts of grass that was their backyard.

"Up here." We looked up to the leaves shaking in the lone maple tree. "I'm up here."

She was up near the top of the tree, even higher than I'd ever dared to climb on anything.

"Come on down so we can go," I said.

Lydia moved down from branch to branch like a monkey and then dropped to the ground. She ran across the yard to the church and returned with a paper sack. "Okay, got my clothes," she said.

Dad was waiting out front and drove us home.

"Boy, y'all got a nice house," she said as we walked inside, through the living and dining areas to the kitchen. Like most older homes it had many small rooms, each with several doors. We didn't keep it as clean and organized as Mom had, but I didn't think it would make much difference to Lydia.

"We used to live in a real house," she said. "I'm not complaining, though."

Dad said we could sleep outside in the old army tent Mr. Kaminsky had given us. We set it up under the trees at the back of the yard, padding the floor with a quilt and blankets. After supper we showed Lydia around town and carried everything we thought we would need out to the tent. I felt like a soldier or an explorer.

We gathered small branches for a fire as the sun went down. I held a match to dry grass and soon the pile of sticks was flaming yellow. We sat around our little fire.

"There's Venus, the evening star," Lydia said, pointing to the sky just above where the sun had set.

"Who taught you that?" I asked. Not many people knew the planets from the stars.

"That's about all I know. Learned it from my grandpa. Sometimes Venus is the morning star."

"That's right. Do you like to read?" I asked.

"I never learned too good. We moved around so much. Mom can't read hardly at all."

"That's terrible," I said.

Lana said, "Hey, she can't help it."

"I didn't mean that." I opened up a bag of potato chips, took out a handful, and passed it to Lydia. We stared at the fire and ate chips. We talked about the kids at school, filling Lydia in.

As the fire died down to white embers, Lydia wiped her hands on her pants, took a harmonica from her pocket, and began to play. It was a sorrowful tune I couldn't place, and it made me feel lonely inside.

I watched Lydia's face in the dim light. She had green eyes and the straightest brown hair that reached almost to her waist, pulled back in a ponytail. But her jeans had a Kmart label and her T-shirt was probably from charity. She lived in an old church with no father and a moody sister. She didn't read. I could sense that sorry feeling coming on me, but I brushed it off. Lydia said she had nothing to complain about, that she liked living there, so why should I feel sorry?

Lydia stopped playing and put the harmonica back in her pocket. We moved into the tent and lay side by side, wrapped in our blankets.

"What's your dad do?" Lydia said from the darkness.

"My dad sells insurance," Lana said.

"My dad's a mechanic and sells used cars," I said. "Sometimes he puts roofs on houses and other work like that. He's going to have his own garage soon."

"My mom started in at the Café and Deb's trying to get on there, too. Then I'll have to babysit more. I like Bobby but he's a pest sometimes."

"Your little brother's cute."

"He ain't my brother. He belongs to Deb."

"Oh," Lana said.

"She ain't old enough, is she?" I said, realizing I had easily slipped into Lydia's dialect.

"She's eighteen." She looked at me as if I'd asked a stupid question.

"What about your dad?" I asked.

"What about him?"

"I mean, what happened? Where is he?"

"Mom said he was good for nothing. We're better off without him. I'm glad he's gone." She rearranged her blanket and pulled it up to her chin.

We grew tired and lay in silence. A dog barked down the street.

The soldiers lay in their tents, thinking of home, mothers, fathers, sweethearts. Even on the battlefield they could hear the familiar sound of frogs and crickets. It almost made them feel like they were back home.

I couldn't go to sleep. I couldn't imagine not having a father. My dad was having some problems right now, but when he was working, with sleeves rolled up, hands on an engine or nailing boards on a roof, it seemed like he could do anything, like he was invincible. He was happiest when he had work to do.

I could hear Lydia's slow, even breathing but I lay wide awake thinking, remembering. One time Dad let me go with him when he poured cement for a driveway. He used the cement mixer that had belonged to his dad. He shoveled in the sand and water and cement powder. It spun around until it was done, and then Dad dumped it out and spread it around with a flat trowel until it was perfectly smooth. When we poured the cement for our own patio a few years ago, he'd let me put my hand in the wet cement before it set and wrote the date next to it, 1965, with a stick.

"We'll always remember this day," he said. "It's set in cement."

He also let me go with him when he worked on the Antorettis' roof. I put on a nail apron and pounded together scrap wood to make what I called animal dwellings. Dad and I ate lunch together out of his metal lunch box. We talked about roofs and tools and the Antorettis. I loved it, but he didn't take me with him again. There wasn't that much for me to do and I was just underfoot, he said. I tried to help him when he worked in the garage, but all I could do was hand him wrenches and tools, often the wrong ones. It wasn't much fun, plus it was dirty and gloomy in the garage.

I wanted to go with him on his volunteer fireman runs, but he said it was against the rules. He said it was serious business and no place for little girls. Since Dad joined the volunteer fire department, a barn burned down, there were some kitchen fires, and some false alarms. Nothing serious. He didn't have to do much as a volunteer fireman except be ready.

In August, right before school started, Remington had its annual Gun Festival and Carnival. People came for the gun show, shooting contests, and exhibits, but the main attraction for me was the carnival downtown. The roads were closed off to make room for rides, contests, and food booths. Country kids would come to town and there was always the hope I would run into Randy or that something interesting would happen.

It was a hot, humid day, and I had a five-dollar bill from Dad in my back pocket to buy a full-day pass for the rides. I took a few quarters from my money jar to buy a Coke and food.

"Jude, I need you to get that fudge from Miss Devore. For the firemen's table," Dad called from the kitchen.

"I'll never get out of her house. You know how she is."

"Better you than me." He smiled.

"And do you think her fudge would be safe to eat?"

"Just go."

I walked the two blocks to old Lela Devore's house and knocked on the door. I could hear her heavy body pressing the floorboards as she crossed the room, her little dog yapping all the way.

She opened the door. "Why, Judy, come on in."

She slammed her leg in front of the dog, "Pierre, shut up, you fool."

She leaned her head down toward me. "I've got some fudge for you, Judy."

"Yeah, that's why I came."

Her house was shut tight as a vault, trapping in the scent of dog. I wanted to leave immediately.

"Come on into the kitchen. I'll get a sack for you." She motioned with her hand for me to follow, then raised her voice. "Pierre, get down. Judy doesn't want you jumping on her." She was right about that.

She shuffled across the kitchen in her slippers and disappeared into the pantry, still talking.

"I've got some sacks in here for that fudge. How're you and your dad doing? And young Marty?"

"Oh, they're okay." I shifted my feet and looked around the kitchen.

Nancy Drew and the Spinster's Clue. Nancy's eyes fell to the little bookshelf by the refrigerator. While the woman was out of sight, Nancy discreetly lifted the layers of random clutter, looking for the elusive clue, the clue to the location of the hidden money.

I stood next to a small drop-leaf table that was covered with an assortment of magazines, mail, a butter dish, a flannel shirt. I noticed what looked like a picture album jutting out from a stack of newspapers. I pulled it out and turned the crinkly plastic pages. Miss Devore wouldn't care. A picture of an old Mr. Devore next to a Studebaker. Some newspaper clippings from the *Renssalaer Rebublican*, yellow with age. "Harsh Winter Sets Records," "City Council Member, Jack Devore, resigns," "Plane Readies for Takeoff from Walstra Farm." "Danny McCool…"

Danny McCool's plane. Serendipity.

A sound like baseballs dropping to the floor came from the pantry followed by, "Shoot!"

"You okay, Miss Devore?"

"Some potatoes got away from me. Stay there, I can get 'em. No room for both of us in here. I can barely turn around."

Ignoring Miss Devore, I read the article about the plane that landed in Remington back in 1938. In the picture a Mr. Devore stood by Danny McCool in front of the plane. The picture was taken as the repaired plane was about to return to Chicago.

"Could you folks use some pickles?" A voice filtered out to me from the pantry.

"Sure."

"I've got bread and butter pickles and dill pickles."

"That's fine. Either one."

Miss Devore appeared from the pantry with a paper bag and some pint jars filled with green. I took the load from her and set it on the kitchen table.

"Do you folks eat hot dogs? I musta got a different brand and I didn't care for 'em." She turned toward the refrigerator.

"We probably don't need any more hot dogs," I said. "But hey, this article here, are you related to the Mr. Devore in the picture? I didn't think you had a husband?"

"That's my brother. Jack. He helped that fool aviator fix his plane."

"Fool?"

"Jack called him a fool. Said the man was just a flash in the pan from Chicago. Said he got some folks angry around here."

"What did he do?"

"I don't know. Let me get those hot dogs." She opened the refrigerator door.

"I need to hurry and get this to the fair."

She found the hot dogs and returned to the table. A plate with little mounds of fudge wrapped in Saran Wrap sat next to a caddy of condiments. She put the fudge in the bag.

"Now, you tell your dad to keep his chin up. He's a good man."

"Okay, Miss Devore."

By the time I finally got out of the house, I had two full sacks, a small one for the firemen's table and a larger one for our family. I ran back home, sacks bouncing against my legs, to find Rita and Lana already there, standing by the car. Lydia, too.

"You did a good thing, Jude," Rita said. She smiled like she often did with her head cocked to the side.

I placed my sack of fudge in the trunk next to Rita's box of baked goods for the Methodist church table. We drove to the fair and unloaded everything.

Then we were free. We bought our all-day passes and went straight to the Tilt-a-Whirl line. From there we worked our way around the circle of entertainment, trying out everything.

I kept one eye open for Randy but didn't see him all day. The previous summer he had come to town with his dad for a farm equipment auction and we had spent a whole afternoon riding bikes around town. We sat on the school swings and talked. He imitated the mannerisms of our teachers and people in town. He was good at it, he made me laugh. He told me stories about working on the farm.

I thought it was something special. It all happened a few months after Mom died, when most of the kids were acting strange around me. Aunt Rita said they just didn't know what to say, but it made me feel like everyone was avoiding me or like something was wrong with me now. Randy wasn't like that. He was friendly and made me forget all the sadness for a while. But once we got back in school that fall, it was like nothing happened at all. I still never gave up hope that he could be my boyfriend.

It was fun being with Lydia, though. I found out she had never been on a carnival ride. When we stopped briefly at the very top of the Ferris wheel, swaying in the air, Lydia leaned forward to point to the field beyond the grain elevator. I grabbed the sides of our swinging car as it pitched forward.

"I need to be at that judging booth at two o'clock. I entered the gun shoot," she said.

I looked at her in surprise. I didn't know any girls who shot guns.

She said, "Ain't anything wrong with that, is there? They said I could enter in the intermediate group."

"No, guess there's nothing wrong with it." The Ferris wheel was moving now. I remembered walking behind my dad rabbit hunting in the woods a couple of times, but he never let me shoot the gun. I had my Swiss Army knife, which I thought was daring enough for a girl, but a gun?

Sure enough, that afternoon, her mom brought her little rifle into town and I watched the contest. For such a skinny girl, she whipped that gun up, sighted down the barrel, and she actually won first place. She beat four boys.

That evening I was almost proud to be with her and Lana as we walked among the noisy crowd. But when I mentioned it to a few friends that Lydia had won the shooting contest, they said congratulations to her, like it was an obligation, and then changed the subject.

Just before Lydia and Lana got in Aunt Rita's car to go home, I asked Lydia if I could shoot her gun sometime and she said, "Sure, come on over anytime." I was already thinking of how it would improve our Robinson Crusoe camp, make it more authentic. Maybe we could shoot a squirrel and cook it outside.

And then Trudy's brother was killed in Vietnam.

CHAPTER 7

October 1938
Wednesday

RUSSELL HANDED DANNY A PAIR OF BLACK OVERBOOTS WITH TWO broken clasps as they dressed by lamplight in the kitchen. "My brother Floyd said you could use these."

The boots were a little tight over Danny's white shoes, but they would work. They walked out to the barn in the early morning darkness.

"We'll go to town after breakfast," he said. Russ knew the corn had to be harvested, but he also knew that parts had to be bought for the plane so this man could move on out of their home. His brothers would work without him this morning.

The sun shone brightly as Russ and Danny traveled the two miles into Remington trailing a cloud of dust. Trees were beginning to take on the reds and yellows of fall. In town they drove right alongside the TP&W railroad tracks, which ran down the middle of the wide main street. Passing C.W. Peck General Store, they parked in front of J.D. Allman Hardware.

Inside the store, Danny picked up the *Remington Republican* newspaper from a pile next to the cash register where J.D. Allman stood watch. He scanned the headlines and then opened the paper wide in front of him, scanning up and down the columns.

"You want to buy that paper, sir?"

"Just glancing." He laid it down. "Do you carry the *Chicago Daily News?*"

Mr. Allman looked down at Danny's gray woolen pant and white shoes. "You're not from around here, are you?"

"No, afraid not."

Russell picked up the paper and placed it back on the stack. "Jim, this here is Danny McCool. He's the fellow that landed the plane out at our place."

"Oh, yeah. I did hear something about that. What can I help you with, Russ?"

"Well, we need some length of pipe, about this size." Russ held out a piece of the landing gear. He handed Mr. Allman a list of items Devore thought they would need.

"And we'd like to buy a radio battery," Danny added.

Mr. Allman helped them around the store until they found the battery, the pipe, some wire, some screws. Danny paid for it all from his envelope of money.

"Too bad you don't get the Chicago paper. Got to keep up with what's going on in the world."

"We get some news in our paper, enough for us." Russ tapped the *Remington Republican.*

"You are aware of what Adolf Hitler is doing. He invaded Austria, you know. A lot of people don't think he's going to stop there."

"Sure, we've heard, but I guess what we're most worried about is the price of corn. Doesn't look like times are ever going to get better around here."

"If we ever go to war again, I'll be there. Fighting from the air." He punched the air as if boxing. "I am a good pilot, you know."

Mr. Allman looked down at the counter.

"Hope it don't come to that," Russell said.

That evening Russell handed Danny a pitchfork as they stood in the horse stall. "Here you go, spread this straw around, so." He picked up a second fork for himself.

"You've got a wonderful family, Russ." Danny leaned on his pitchfork.

"Wanted to do better by them," Russ said, jabbing at the straw.

"I really did want to marry Jean. I've had lots of girls wanted to marry me, but she was the first one I felt that way about. Not used to such bad luck. Girls like aviators, you know."

"Don't know," Russ said. "Got married right before '29, things were looking good, thought I'd make money fast, build up the farm, see."

"Rotten luck," Danny said.

"Mary's used to better. Her family's French, Mary Lorraine Fontaine was her name. Grew up in a nice home, had nice things. She's not real strong, hard on her to have to work like this."

Ellen appeared at the doorway just then, holding a pumpkin bigger than a basketball. Her face almost glowed.

"Mother said I could pick it. And there's more out in the garden. We're going to make pies." She held the pumpkin up like a trophy and then turned toward the house.

Danny said, "I want to have a family like you someday. Find me another woman." He waved his arm toward the open barn door. "I like this open country, myself. The fresh air, pumpkins."

"You don't really know nothing about it," Russell said.

That evening Russell put the new battery in the radio. The girls had already gone to bed. "I'm starved for news," Danny said as he knelt next to the Philco, twisting the knobs in search of a strong radio signal. Russell and Mary watched from the davenport nearby. He stopped when *The National Barn Dance* came through loud and clear followed by a news broadcast. Danny sat down and leaned toward the radio. The announcer reported that a few days before, England's Prime Minister Chamberlain had signed a non-aggression pact with Germany. Chamberlain promised peace for our time.

"Well, how about that," Danny said. "Peace for our time." He pulled a handkerchief out of his shirt pocket, tossed it toward the ceiling, and snatched it on the way down. "Hooray!"

CHAPTER 8

Summer 1968

I KNEW THERE WAS A WAR IN VIETNAM BECAUSE I HEARD ABOUT IT ON TV. Sometimes adults talked about it, but it didn't mean much to me until Steven Kaminsky was killed in active duty. We had to go to the funeral. It was an obligation.

I had only been to two other funerals. The first one was for Grandpa Walstra, who died a few years before, but he was old, even though everyone said he was way too young to die of a stroke. It was the first time I saw someone dead in a casket, face like wax, powdered and made up. I saw my mom cry and I cried, too. And then there was Mom's funeral. Thinking about it now, her funeral seems like a scene from a movie about someone else. People patted us on the back and hugged us and told us it was normal to feel so numb after a tragedy like that. They said that's why we felt like we were in a fog with bees buzzing in our ears, and why we sometimes felt nothing at all, and why sometimes we cried like babies.

Dad and Marty and I knew we had to go to Steven's funeral no matter how hard it was. The Kaminskys were our neighbors, and it was just one of those times when we had to get back on the horse.

Dad put on his dark gray suit that he just wore to weddings and funerals, and Marty put on his best shirt with his black pants. I put on my striped blue dress with the belt at the dropped waist, and we all got ready in silence. We had to wait in line just to get in the doors for the viewing, so it took forever. It seemed like the whole town was there. I fidgeted as we moved forward, listening as people whispered around me. Kingston Funeral Home smelled of roses, which was the smell of death to me.

The Kingstons actually lived in one part of the home and had a son my age. When we were about six years old, Mrs. Kingston had a birthday party for Robby and I was invited. When Mom found out the party was going to be right there in the funeral home, in the big front room where they have the visitations, she said, "You're not going to a birthday party in a funeral home."

Dad said, "I'm sure there won't be any dead people there at the party, Blue Jay." He laughed and winked at me.

Mom said, "It's not funny. I can't believe they're having a party for little kids where my own father lay in death."

I didn't get to go.

When we finally got into the room where the Kaminskys were, they looked diminished and pale as they stood by their son's casket. Trudy and her brother Nick sat in chairs behind them. A row of extended Kaminsky family members stood nearby.

"I don't know what to say," I whispered to Dad.

"Just say 'I'm sorry'."

Steven's face looked fuller, but I could tell it was him. I didn't stand there long, but moved quickly on.

After saying "I'm sorry," to each of the Kaminskys in turn, I almost felt like it was my fault. Trudy shook when I hugged her. It was so awkward. I didn't know what else to say to her. Again I said, "I'm sorry."

"I need to go to the bathroom," I told Dad. It was too much. I needed to get out of there.

I quickly moved through the crowd, squeezing sideways between people, went to the bathroom, then out onto the porch where men were smoking and talking. I sat in one of the empty rocking chairs. It was still hot and humid even at eight thirty. I rocked and listened to the old men in order to change the subject in my mind.

One of the men said, "It's just a shame. I mean, I honor these boys that give their lives, but I'm just afraid it's all for nothing. It's not a good cause. Not like World War Two." He raised his right hand and jabbed his finger into the air. "Now, that was a good cause. Those men were true heroes."

I thought about Danny McCool. He was the only WWII hero I knew about.

"This boy was still a hero in my eyes," the other man continued.

"I'm not saying he wasn't a hero. I'll honor him, like I said. But I'm just saying the war itself isn't right. Maybe we should bring those boys home."

"Now, where would we be if we'd said that in forty-four?"

I leaned back in the rocker. After what had happened to Steven Kaminsky, I didn't suppose Trudy would want to join us when we went to Lydia's to shoot guns.

I waited a few days before I decided it would be a good idea to take something to the Kaminskys. Right after Mom died, people brought us all sorts of casseroles and sandwiches and desserts. We were inundated with food. It was nice knowing people were thinking about us. Since Trudy didn't avoid me during that time, I thought I shouldn't avoid her, even though death does make you want to run the other way.

I looked through the kitchen cupboards and found a brownie mix behind some cans of vegetables. I followed the directions and soon the kitchen smelled like it did when Mom used to make desserts. I cut the brownies in squares, put them on a nice glass plate, and covered it with foil. I walked across the yard to the Kaminskys' house, past all the decorations to the front door. To keep from getting too nervous, I examined the gray shingle siding, the white trim, the red front door, the loose gutter at the left-hand corner of the roof, when suddenly Trudy opened the door.

"Hi, Trudy." I pushed the plate into her hands.

"Hey, Jude."

I stepped up and hugged her. "You want to come in?" she asked.

I stepped into the dim interior. Trudy's mom was sitting on the couch watching a game show on TV, but she turned it off when I came in.

"Nice to see you, Judy," she said, but she wasn't her usual cheerful self. She was totally bland, but that was to be expected. They both just looked at me.

"I made you some brownies. You can keep the plate for a while. Where's Mr. Kaminsky?"

"He had to go back to work, dear."

I looked around the room. A stack of clean casserole dishes sat on the table. It brought back memories of Grandma Walstra washing the dishes people had brought us. Sympathy cards lay at various places around the room. This was harder than I thought it would be.

"Uh, I thought you might like some brownies. I made them myself."

It was so was awkward, but then I had an idea.

"Trudy, do you want to go downtown and walk around?"

She jumped up. "Yes."

Her mom said, "Yes, that would be good for her."

So we walked up and down, street after street, even though it was hot. I kept asking Trudy questions and got her talking about her brother, and she told me how bad she felt, and how her parents felt guilty, and she cried and it made me cry, too. But I think it was good for her and maybe for me, too, like a catharsis.

We stopped by the old wooden water tower downtown and sat on the bench to rest. There was one story I knew would make Trudy laugh so I thought I'd bring it up.

"Trudy. Remember the time we drove our bikes out in the country and got in trouble?"

She wiped her eye and managed a little smile. "Yeah, Dad flipped out on that one."

Trudy actually babysat me for a short time a few years ago—until this incident happened. She was twelve and I was eight. Dad worked at the elevator, Mom's hours changed at the library, and Marty had track practice, so there were a couple times a week when I was home alone after school. The Kaminskys offered for Trudy to babysit. She would fix me a snack and we'd watch TV or snoop around Marty's room for fun.

It was early spring at the time. The snow was gone, purple hyacinths were popping up, feelings of adventure were beginning to stir. Trudy thought we should get outside and ride our bikes.

I said, "Are you sure? Should we leave our house?"

"Mom said I was in charge. Let's do it."

We got our bikes out of storage. The Kaminskys didn't even notice. We headed into the country where there'd be less traffic. We pedaled to 1800 South, turned left, went to the next country road, and turned left again. The sun beamed onto our backs. We stopped awhile at Carpenters Creek, which was running full after spring rains. We were careful on the road and only met a few cars, but the trip took longer than we thought it would. When we got back, Dad was about to call the police since no one knew where we were. They were so relieved to see us. It turned out Mom and Dad took it better than Mr. Kaminsky. He was furious at Trudy.

Trudy smiled at the memory. "Yeah, Dad took my bike apart and threw the pieces to the back of the shed behind the Christmas decorations. We never did find all the parts and put it back together. I didn't have a bike for two years."

I remember you said to him, "You told me I was in charge."

"Yeah, that didn't help my case any," she said, turning to me with one eyebrow raised.

It was good to see Trudy laugh, even though her eyes were puffy from crying. "We had fun that day, didn't we?"

"Yeah, we did." We sat awhile in silence.

When we got back to the house, Trudy stopped on the steps.

"Thanks for coming over, Jude. I feel a little better."

As I lay in bed that night, I felt like I'd done a good deed and helped myself at the same time, but my thoughts soon shifted to school—the fact that it started in three weeks and the fact that I didn't have enough new clothes. Dad didn't know how to shop for girl's things, so Aunt Rita had taken me shopping with Lana before Steven's funeral. I got some new shoes, new underwear, and one new dress to start sixth grade. But that definitely wouldn't be enough.

A week later, a second new family moved to town. Lana and I were on the scene, straddling our bikes in front of the *Glass House,* the one with the sharp-angled modern design, entire walls made of glass panels. It had sat empty for over a year. We watched two men struggle with a refrigerator in the back of the Mayflower van while another worker rolled a wooden desk up the sidewalk on a cart.

We could see right into the house. A woman in tight pink pants pointed to a wall, directing the placement of the desk. A girl about our age with a blond ponytail sat first on one chair, then another, opened and shut closet doors, then left the room. In the backyard an older boy in plaid shorts sat in a patio chair, legs stretched out in front of him.

"Interesting," I said.

"They're rich," Lana said.

"Of course they are. Look at their clothes and furniture. I bet they're stuck-up."

We continued to watch until someone suddenly pulled the drapes shut.

We rode back to my house, laid the bikes on the ground, and stepped onto the porch. Dad leaned against the railing reading the *TV Guide.*

"We watched that new family move in, over on Fifth Street," I said.

"James Wilson the second," Dad said, slapping the *TV Guide* against the palm of his hand. "He's the big lawyer, now. He swore he'd never come back to Remington, but I guess he wasn't doing so well in Fort Wayne."

Dad picked up his cup of coffee, which sat on the windowsill.

"Yep, decided to join his dad's law firm in Renssalaer after all. Now it's Wilson, Wilson, and O'Polka." He emphasized the second Wilson. "Went to school with him."

"I think they have a girl our age," I said.

"Probably do." He walked into the house.

CHAPTER 9

October 1938
Thursday

DANNY JOINED RUSSELL AND HIS BROTHERS TO HELP WITH THE CORN picking on Thursday. Russell was putting him to good use while he stayed here, Danny reasoned. Until Devore could help with the plane repairs and get the fuel, they were at a standstill anyway.

Corn picking was exhausting work. The men walked between the rows, stripped each ear of corn from the stalk, removed the the husks with the help of a peg strapped to their glove, and then threw the ears against the bang board and into the wagon. The horse walked slowly, but Danny still had trouble keeping up.

When the wagon was full, Russell and Danny drove into Remington. The corncrib was full so this load would go to the elevator. They pulled up to the front of the grain elevator, a four-story wooden building next to the railroad tracks. Birds picked at the grain that littered the ground and perched in rows on the telephone lines overhead. A man in blue overalls and straw hat walked out onto the wooden platform that ran like a porch the length of the building. He stood at the far end of the platform as Russ lined up the wagon.

"Hey, Harold," Russell called out.

Harold waved his hand like a salute for Russ to go ahead. You could tell they had done this before.

Russ grabbed the two shovels wedged next to the sideboard and handed one to Danny, who sagged against the side of the wagon.

"Guess you're going to help, buddy," Harold said. Danny caught him winking at Russell as he lifted up the trapdoor in the platform.

Danny climbed onto the wagon and pushed the shovel under the dry ears, then heaved the corn into the bin under the trapdoor. He'd show these men what he could do, though he tossed one load for every two of Russell's. He leaned on the shovel after several minutes and looked toward the top of the elevator.

"I suppose an auger lifts this corn up there." He pointed to a fluttering blue flag at the top of the building.

"Yep," Russ said, sending another shovelful down the chute.

Danny looked to Harold, who added, "Once your corn gets up there, my brother, Herb, will pull a rope that sends it into the right bin for storage. Later on it'll go down another chute, where it gets shelled, bagged, or shipped away on the railroad to Chicago."

"I'm from Chicago, you know."

"That's what I hear," Harold said, rolling a cigarette, not looking up.

When the wagon was empty, they stepped up onto the platform and entered the office, where several cats lay asleep. Danny sucked in the heady smell of grain. He walked straight to a mound of sacks plump with feed and sat down, scanning the advertisements that covered the walls like peeling wallpaper. Russ stood by the counter nearby until Harold handed him several bills from the cash box. Russ recounted the money and put it in his pocket.

"So, you're the aviator that landed in Russ's field," Harold said, scanning Danny from head to foot. He must appear an outsider even in the borrowed work clothes.

"That's me."

"This here is my brother, Herb," Harold said. He jerked his thumb toward the dimness behind the counter where a man in similar overalls sat at a small table by an unlit stove. He appeared to be the older of the two, but it may have been his beard, which was streaked with gray.

He looked up just long enough to offer a nod and then shuffled a deck of cards and laid them on the table next to a jumble of coffee cups.

Russ said, "Hey now, Danny, why don't you show these fellas those card tricks you showed the girls."

Danny walked around the counter, picked up the worn deck from the table, shuffled the cards once, and fanned them out in front of the brothers. Herb picked at his teeth with a splinter of wood while Harold stood nearby. He performed the card trick as he had done for the girls.

"You a card player?" Herb asked.

"I've played."

"Now, do that trick again so I can watch you close," Harold said. "How'd you do that?"

"Can't share my secrets, now, can I?" Danny stood up straight and placed the cards firmly on the table.

"We know a few tricks ourselves, huh, Herb?" He looked toward his brother.

"You fellas play poker?" Danny asked, noticing the box of poker chips on the shelf.

"All the time, except when we're working or there's ladies around." They laughed.

"You any good?" Herb asked.

"Not bad. Want to play a hand?"

Russ interrupted, "Why don't you stay here, see, while I go put this money in the bank and stop by the blacksmith. I want Butch to take a look at the chestnut's foot. Noticed it limping a little today. I'll come back and pick you up."

Harold nodded and Russ left. By the time he got back, they were still at it. Danny thought they must have appeared like old poker buddies to Russell, slapping down cards, laughing. Danny felt like he was winning them over.

"Getting any work done, boys?" Russ said with a little laugh.

"We sent our boy Frank out to take care of that," said Harold. "Your man Danny is good, but Herb always wins. Like usual."

Herb leaned onto the back legs of his chair and ran his hand through his beard.

"What can I say?" he said.

"Well, got to break this game up, there's chores to do."

"Thanks, fellas," said Danny. "Maybe later?"

"Try us on Saturday night. We go over to the back room in Shooter's Bar. We meet Ray and Big Mike over there."

"Okay. Maybe I'll take you up on that." They shook hands all around and left.

CHAPTER 10

Fall 1968

SCHOOL STARTED WHETHER WE WERE READY OR NOT. LANA AND I sat with Lydia at lunch because we wanted to help her fit in. I noticed that Lydia was wearing some of Lana's old clothes, and I wondered if anyone else noticed. No one seemed to care that she won that shooting contest at the fair.

Within the first week I could tell it wasn't going to work. The accent that I'd admired, and even slipped into at times, was made fun of by the other kids. They called Lydia a hillbilly. Lana stuck by her, but I found myself pulling back. Kids were just starting to treat me like a normal person again, and I didn't want to jeopardize that.

Our teacher, Mrs. Clark, tried to make Lydia feel welcome. Mrs. Clark was new to the school herself; this was only her second year. She wore pretty dresses every day with a pearl necklace at her throat. She was tough on the troublemakers in class, but I liked her because she made class interesting. Her round face often broke into a smile defined in red lipstick. She made sure when she assigned groups for the diorama project that Lydia would be with people most likely to accept her. So she put Lydia with Lana and me. I felt sorry for Lydia but not enough to have her ruin my year. I was determined to make the best of sixth grade. We were the oldest students in the building, after all. Trudy said sixth grade was the best and after that things got worse. And she should know.

Lydia wasn't the only new student that year. Kristy Wilson, the girl who lived in the *Glass House*, was also in our class and she really shook things up. She upset the balance of power. It seemed like Kristy's name carried more weight because her dad was a lawyer. At first I thought it was childish how everyone was falling over themselves trying to win her favor. The girls revolved around her like planets, and the boys would do things like trip each other in the hall or brag during class and then look to see if she was watching. I didn't want to demean myself like that, but I found myself more and more isolated with Lana and Lydia at the lunch table. I decided I needed to make some changes.

One change I'd already made was to join Band. I had a free instrument, my clarinet, so Dad said to go ahead. I knew Randy was in Band, but I was surprised to see Kristy there holding a trumpet, of all things.

When I told Lana, she said, "She just plays the trumpet because the rest of the trumpet players are boys."

"It's a free country," I said. "What's wrong with that?"

Lana wasn't even in Band, which I thought was a little surprising since her real dad was a musician. Maybe things like that weren't always hereditary.

We had Band once a week across the street in the old high school. Oscar Nicholson, the band teacher, towered over us. Everything about him was long and thin, his face, his legs, his arms, his fingers. He told the students he could play every one of the instruments in the band. He talked to me at the end of class when everyone was putting their instruments away.

"Judy, I taught your mother when she was in this high school. You look a lot like her, by the way," he said. "And this is a beautiful instrument." He took the clarinet from my hands. "It's older, but the wonderful craftsmanship is obvious." He turned it over in his hands and held it like a tiny baby. He handed it back to me so I could put it in its case.

"If you stay after school once a week, I'll soon have you up to speed with the rest of the students. Most of them started Band last year, but there are a few others like you who need to catch up."

It was a fun class. I caught on quickly and learned to make a smooth clean sound, without squeaks or squawks. A lot depended on a fresh, properly aligned reed. I liked the complexity of the keys.

Kristy didn't seem to take her trumpet too seriously. Sometimes I think she messed up just to get attention or so she could ask the boys for advice. She liked to laugh and point out the pink circle around her mouth after she'd played for a while. "Look," she'd say, pursing her lips at the boys. Maybe I needed to be a little sillier to get the attention of the boys. Maybe I could learn some things from her.

Randy played snare drums and the bass drum. I went up to him and said, "You've got the easiest instrument of all. All you have to do is pound on that big old drum."

"Are you kidding? Mr. Nicholson said I've got the most important job of all—keeping the beat. If I goof up we'll all be offbeat. He says the drums are like the foundation of a house." He placed his hands on top of each other like he was laying bricks. I picked up a drumstick and hit a snare drum. He took the sticks away from me, but he was smiling.

"Bet you couldn't play the clarinet," I said, shaking my head at him. This was the way we joked around in Band. I was still trying to get Randy's attention.

"We can't drive across town to church without you kids getting in a fight," Dad said, slapping his hand against the steering wheel. "Can't go one mile without a fight."

We still went to church almost every Sunday. Mom had always been the faithful one, but Dad was doing his best to keep it up out of respect for her. This particular Sunday the problem started before we even got in the truck. Marty woke up at the last minute, so we both needed the bathroom at the same time and I had to wait on him and then rush to get ready. I climbed into the truck, still upset, and took my usual spot wedged between Dad and Marty in the cab of the truck.

Dad backed up and we started down the street. "When was the last time you washed your hair?" Marty said.

"I could not wash my hair this morning." I glared at him. "I couldn't even get in the bathroom. You always get your way in everything."

Things just went downhill from there. We threw insults back and forth. Marty grabbed my wrist and twisted it hard. I squealed and slammed against Dad's arm.

"Dad, stop him. He's hurting me."

Dad reached across me and swatted at Marty, causing the truck to swerve. "Dammit, would you shut up and stop your fighting? I lost your mother, and now you two do nothing but fight."

We were shocked. We had never heard Dad curse before. It was quiet the rest of the way to church.

I thought back to the way Mom tried to quiet down our arguments by giving us each a stick of gum. That would just upset Dad, and he'd say, "Don't reward them for arguing. They need to learn to get along."

"I'm not rewarding them," she'd say. "I just thought it would help, that's all."

One time he was so upset that he stopped the car. "I'm not going to church like this." He got out of the car and walked home. We all felt rotten, but Mom composed herself and told us to shape up. She drove us around the block, and by the time we walked up the steps to the church's red front door, we were all smiling, at least on the outside. Mom and Dad just had different ways of dealing with things.

This particular Sunday, after Dad swore, we were all back to neutral when we arrived at the Methodist church. It was a sturdy brick building that looked like a castle with stained-glass windows that curved upward to a point. We reached the steps where Pastor Landaur stood.

"Morning, kids. Morning, Mr. James. Beautiful day today."

"Morning, Pastor Landauer. Yes, it is," said Dad.

By this time Marty had moved ahead through the door and turned to the left to sit with the teenage boys on the back row. Dad and I turned to the right and found our seat about halfway toward the front where we always sat. Already I felt the calming effect of being in the church, organ music in the background, soft light filtering in through the stained-glass windows. The church sat in the center of Remington, completed in 1917, and offering its hope to the people all around it ever since. I felt "the presence of the Lord," as Mom described it.

I used to help Mom clean the church once a month when it was her turn, and even then I felt that same comforting feeling. My job was to dust the wooden pews, make sure the hymnals were in place, and gather up all the used bulletins and gum wrappers. While she was cleaning the bathrooms and Sunday school rooms, I would sit at the piano and pick out the melody to "Amazing Grace" or try to play Beatles songs like "Let It Be." I stood behind the wooden pulpit, barely able to see over the top, and looked out over the empty pews.

Reverend Jude stood before the crowd, voice ringing out like a bell. "Jesus said, 'Stand up and be counted. Defend the fatherless and widows. Bring Me your huddled masses.'" She raised her fist and brought it down onto the pulpit. "I have a dream." A hundred amens flew up from the crowd. Reverend Jude gathered her robes around her and picked up her Bible. "Go in peace and God bless you."

Being in the church always made me feel better.

After the opening hymn, we were dismissed for Sunday school and then returned to our seats for the main service. By then I had completely forgotten the argument in the car. Lately, instead of daydreaming or coloring pictures from our Sunday school papers, I was actually listening to Pastor Landaur's messages. This morning he was talking about loving our neighbor and not judging people by outward appearances.

"We may say we are not prejudiced. It's easy to say we have no prejudice against colored people when there are no colored people in our community. But prejudice comes in many forms. We may be prejudiced against poor people, or people with a handicap, or people who don't believe like we do." He swept his hand over the crowd, but I felt like he was pointing to me. "You children and teenagers may be prejudiced against your fellow classmates who aren't as popular or who don't have as nice clothes. Jesus said not to judge by the outward appearance."

I no longer felt that comforting feeling. I felt like Pastor Landauer was referring to me. I thought about Lydia. The kids were making fun of her like they made fun of Priscilla, the biggest girl in class who was already getting acne, who wore tight polyester skirts and shirts that looked like they belonged to her mom. I thought of old Herb. Kids avoided him and said mean things about him, said he was crazy and dangerous. It would be hard to do what the pastor was saying. I'd have to think about it.

As we filed out of church, Pastor Landauer gripped Dad's hands in his. He seemed genuinely concerned from the look in his eyes.

"How are things going for you, R.J.?"

"Things are fine," Dad said.

I knew the pastor thought Dad should get remarried, like a lot of people did. But Dad wasn't so sure. He did go on one date this past winter on the advice of Uncle Phil, of all people. Phil told Dad about this woman he worked with who was divorced, no kids.

"She'd be perfect for you, R.J."

Her name was Alice. She seemed nice, had a pretty smile and curly hair, but she and Dad had one date, went to a movie in Rensselaer, and that was that.

"She's not my style," he said.

I agreed with Dad when he told people we were fine. I wasn't ready for another woman to come into our house.

On Monday Lana and Lydia ended up sitting with me at lunch. I knew I shouldn't judge her, especially after what the pastor said, but it didn't mean she had to be my best friend. I shouldn't have to eat with her every day. We sat on the bleachers during lunch recess to watch the boys shoot baskets on the gym floor. Everyone around us was in sixth grade or younger.

"We rule this school," I said.

"I don't feel like I rule anything," said Lydia.

Lana put her hand on her arm. "It'll get better. You're still new."

Lana turned to me. "I guess we better enjoy whatever rule we have now. Next year we'll go to Tri-County Junior High and have to start all over. Trudy said it's the pits in seventh grade."

She handed me and Lydia a square of Hershey's chocolate.

"Don't ruin it. We still rule this year," I said.

"No, Kristy rules the school." She spit the words out and pointed down to the gym floor.

I watched Kristy Wilson shooting baskets with the boys, and it definitely wasn't because she was any good at basketball.

Lana said, "She isn't even that pretty, but she's popular because she's rich and has nice clothes."

"She's not bad just because she's popular," I said.

Lana went on, "And don't forget her dad is a lawyer. She's always reminding everyone of that. She just tries out different girls and boys as friends until she gets tired of them and then spits them out like old chewing gum." She folded up the rest of her Hershey bar and stuffed it in her jacket pocket, like that was the last word on the subject.

I decided then and there I had to be Kristy's friend. I was getting tired of Lana the do-gooder. And Pastor Landaur had apparently forgotten what it was like to be in school. Anyway, prejudice could go both ways, couldn't it? Wasn't Lana being prejudiced against Kristy? It was clear now that Lydia, with her old used clothes and Kentucky accent, didn't fit in and Lana didn't seem to care, but if I was ever going to be more popular and attract the boys, I needed new friends. Trudy said that in junior high it was all about being popular. Not that Trudy was that popular herself, but she was older and knew what she was talking about.

It was the strangest thing, but what brought me and Kristy together was my own brother, Marty. I was hanging up my coat at the back of the classroom one Tuesday morning and Kristy came up to me.

"Is Marty James your brother?"

I hesitated and then said, "Yes."

I didn't know if this was a good thing or a bad thing. I knew Marty had been hanging around with Kristy's brother, the one I'd seen in the yard the day they moved in. From overhearing Marty, I knew her brother's name was Brad and that they shot baskets together and that he let Marty drive him around in his car. For some reason Brad had a car but didn't have his license.

Kristy continued, "Marty's so cute. I just love him." So this was a good thing. I relaxed.

"Hey, Jude, why don't you come to my house Friday," she said. "I'm having a slumber party."

"Sure. Neat! I'm sure I can come."

It was just that easy and I was in.

I waited until after school and then stopped Lana before she joined Lydia on the bus. I knew I had to tell her.

"Kristy invited me to a slumber party this Friday," I said in a normal voice. I didn't want to sound too excited.

Lana swung around at me. "She did?" Her eyes were big. She looked surprised and angry.

"Don't get mad. She'll probably invite you next time. I think she has parties all the time."

"I don't want to go to her old parties or be friends with her." She started toward the bus, but I grabbed her sleeve.

"Why are you so against her?"

"She's just stuck-up and her family's all messed up. You know why they moved here, don't you?"

"What do you mean?"

"Mom said Kristy's mom had a nervous breakdown in Fort Wayne and they thought it would be healthy for her to move here. And she's an alcoholic. A bad alcoholic."

"So? I'm not turning down an opportunity."

I saw how hurt Lana looked, so I backed off. "Okay, I'll just check things out."

"Don't turn into her, Jude."

"I won't." I let go of her sleeve and she got on the bus. I saw her sit down next to Lydia.

It wasn't my fault Kristy invited me and not Lana.

After school on Friday I went home to get my overnight bag and then went straight to Kristy's house for the slumber party. Dad said he didn't care if I went. "While you're there, snoop around and see what a big lawyer's life looks like." He threw some junk mail in the trash and laughed to himself.

"You mean, you want me to look for something, like to solve a mystery?"

"No, I'm just talking. We're not living in a mystery novel. Have a good time, Blue Jay."

Kristy's sidekick, Rhonda, in white leather boots, opened the door for me when I rang the bell at the Wilsons' house. Rhonda was the kind of girl who was overweight but made up for it by getting a dark tan. Stephanie arrived soon afterward and then Carol, another first-timer like me.

I was interested in seeing the inside of the *Glass House*. I had ridden by on my bike from time to time and had seen the swanky furniture in the front room, green drapes always pulled back so anyone could look inside, but that was all. Apparently they didn't spend much time in that front room. It was a room just for looks, superfluous.

Kristy took us to her bedroom to change out of our school clothes. Her room was dominated by a full-size bed with a flowered canopy and matching bedspread. The curtains matched, too. Posters of the

Beatles and Monkees covered the walls. I put on my blue jeans and a black long-sleeved shirt and laid out my new flannel nightgown, new since last Christmas. Kristy pulled on striped bell bottoms and a pink sweater the color of Pepto-Bismol. Her nice clothes and long blond hair took the attention away from her small eyes and pointy nose.

"Where did you get all those dolls, Kristy?" I pointed to the collection of dolls displayed on three shelves above her dresser, probably twenty-five dolls. I was amazed.

"My dad gets them for me when he travels to other cities." I was also impressed by her closet that was like a small room in itself filled with clothes and shoes. I must have looked like an idiot staring at the colorful array because I caught her looking at me like she was about to laugh. I decided to act like it was no big deal, like I had a closet of clothes like that, too.

I pointed to her green sweater. "I have a sweater kinda like that one." It was the best comment I could think of.

She showed us around her house, which was enormous, and I met her mom and dad. Mr. Wilson didn't look like a lawyer, but it was probably because he didn't have his suit on. Mrs. Wilson, like Kristy, had blond hair falling smoothly down her back, and looked slim in a blue-and-gold-striped shirt that she wore untucked over tight navy pants. She seemed normal to me, just a little nervous. Kristy pointed out Brad, who was watching TV in the living room, but he didn't say anything to us and left before supper.

Mrs. Wilson cooked us hamburgers and frozen French fries, which she baked in the oven, then we played card games and made some prank phone calls from Kristy's bedroom. I was beginning to feel like part of the group. Kristy was great.

At midnight Kristy declared she was starving. Her mom was still awake in the family room watching Johnny Carson and seemed happy to bring us a plate of ham sandwiches and bottles of Coke so we could stay up late watching TV. Kristy was the only person I knew of who had her own TV in her bedroom, or who got to stay up so late.

At one o'clock we were all rolled up in blankets on the floor when Kristy said, "I dare us to sneak out."

Rhonda, who always agreed with Kristy, said, "Sure. Let's go. How about to the grain elevator?"

Carol wasn't so sure. "We'd be in big trouble if we get caught out there."

"There is nothing to do in this town, girls. It's nothing like Fort Wayne, where I grew up. You have to make your own excitement here."

Nothing truer had ever been said. Here was my chance for adventure and the way to make Kristy my friend. "I'm in," I said without any further thought.

We persuaded Carol.

At one thirty in the morning we put on our shoes and pulled on our jackets over our pajamas instead of getting dressed because Kristy said it would be more daring that way. We climbed one at a time through Kristy's bedroom window and dropped to the ground. We snuck from bush to building to tree in the dark. The air was chilly, the sky dark and partly cloudy. It was only five blocks to the elevator, but there were streetlights and we would have to cross the broad expanse of Railroad Street. There was always the chance a police car would drive by and see us.

"We actually have to touch the grain elevator or it won't count," Kristy said.

This was great. With the help of my new friends, I felt this was the right thing to do to change my image. I felt more alive than any other time in my life.

The group of five prisoners had escaped the prison, but now they had to get past the guardhouse to reach safety. The searchlight was swinging back toward them so they took cover behind the low wall.

We crouched behind a low hedge as a car with shining headlights moved down the street.

"Okay, now," Kristy whispered loudly.

We crossed New York Street and hurried to the first alley, where it would be darker. This should take us down close to the elevator.

We walked behind Kingman's Funeral Home, feeling bolder all the time. We jumped as the Kingsmans' black dog started barking.

"Run," Kristy said more loudly.

"No, that'll make him bark worse," I said. But no one heard me. I walked fast to catch up. The dog was on a chain and eventually stopped barking.

When we got to Railroad Street we stopped, pressed to the side of the Laundromat. We waited for a car to pass. It seemed the coast was clear, but brightly lit.

We waited on Kristy, who was definitely in charge.

"Do you do this often?" I asked.

"Sure, all the time. And never been caught. We go different places each time."

"Okay. Go," she said.

We ran across the wide expanse of Railroad Street without incident, without tripping on the rails, and then circled all the way around the elevator to the darkness behind. We stopped to catch our breath by the new grain dryer, which roared in the night. Chaff and dust floated in the air, lit up by the pale glow from the security light at the top of the elevator.

"Did you know these elevators can explode? Because of the all the grain dust," I said.

The three girls turned to face me at once. "Really?" Kristy asked.

"Yeah, the dust from the grain can mix with oxygen and create a chain reaction like a bomb. So don't light a match." I could always contribute facts in any situation.

Rhonda spoke up, "Are you a scientist or something?" She laughed.

"My dad used to work here. He said you really have to be careful."

"What happened? Did he get fired?" It was like she was trying to start an argument.

"He just got tired of it, okay?"

"Come on," Kristy said. "We have to leave our mark here on the wall." She patted the sides of her jacket. "Heck, I forgot something to write with."

I produced my Swiss Army knife from my inner jacket pocket. "We could use this," I said, holding it out to Kristy.

She looked at me with surprise. I wasn't sure if it was admiration or ridicule. "You always carry a knife?" she asked.

"Sure. You never know when you might need it." In fact, I did usually carry it with me. Marty found it in the creek but only a few of the blades worked, so he gave it to me.

"You're different," she said. "I like that." I took that as a compliment and looked Rhonda in the eyes. Was she jealous?

We walked over to the elevator, whose wooden walls loomed upward three stories.

"What do you want me to carve?" I had the blade out ready to go.

"Let's put the number five on the wall since there are five of us," Kristy said, holding up her hand with five fingers stretched out.
I put the point of the blade against the wood and scratched out a crude five. I stepped back and looked at my work.

"We're done here," Kristy said.

We edged around to the front of the elevator where the light was bright and waited for Kristy to signal us to go. We went back the same way and made it back through Kristy's window without a hitch. The whole adventure took us less than half an hour. I felt exhilarated. We stayed up until four o'clock and then slept in until eleven the next morning.

"How'd your party go?" Dad asked as I came through the door at lunchtime. He was smearing mayonnaise on his bread, and Marty was opening a pack of bologna.

"Okay. I like their house."

"I don't think I'd like all those big glass windows," Marty said. "People could see right inside your house."

"They never use that room."

"What good's a room you don't use?"

"For company, I guess. Rich people can do that."

Marty snorted as he picked up his sandwich and left the room.

Dad ignored my comment. "Blue Jay, you and Lana are going to help get Grandma's yard ready for winter today before it gets any colder. I've got that little roofing job to finish up at the grocery store and then I'll be out to help."

"All right." I didn't tell him I'd been up most of the night and just wanted to go back to sleep.

Aunt Rita picked me up and we drove the short distance out to the Walstra farm. When we pulled in the drive, we saw Grandma standing by the outdoor faucet in her blue jeans filling buckets with water. She assigned Lana and me the job of putting all the lawn furniture in the garage, while she and Aunt Rita washed windows.

We walked to the patio and hoisted heavy metal chairs over our backs.

"Well?" Lana stared at me. I could tell she was irritated.

"I had fun. It was just a slumber party."

She waited, apparently wanting more information.

"We did do something fun, though."

We started to walk toward the garage.

"We snuck out at night and went down to the grain elevator. It was a blast. We should try it sometime, ourselves."

"I don't know. We wouldn't want to get caught. So that's the kind of things she does at these parties?"

"Sure. She said they never get caught."

We stacked the chairs in the garage and returned for the table.

Lana looked across the table at me. "I'm not mad. I just don't trust her, and I don't want you to stop being my friend because of her."

"Don't worry, we're cousins."

I meant what I said, but I was beginning to feel different. A cousin is family, not like other friends. Summer in the country was one kind of fun, but being at Kristy's house was another kind of fun. I felt like I was two different people, one at school and one with family.

"So is Lydia your best friend now?" I asked.

"She's my friend. I want to help her."

"Why do you feel like you have to help everybody?"

"I don't try to help everybody."

"Okay, I know. But look, you can give Lydia your clothes to wear, but I don't think she's ever going to fit in. You're not going to be able to change the way she talks or the fact that she lives in a church."

"I know. But I can help her, I think." We lifted the metal table between us and started for the garage.

"I've been thinking about it," I said. "It's like when we found that rabbit."

"The one Dad hit with the lawn mower?"

"Yes, that little rabbit. We tried to keep it alive, fix its leg, but Aunt Rita said you can't save every animal."

"I know. Poor little Jumping Bean."

"Maybe Lydia is like that rabbit."

"That's not even the same thing at all," she said. We had reached the garage and we set the table down with a thud.

We didn't talk much more as we carried storm windows out of the barn and placed them by the house for Dad to install later. We moved some rocks and raked some leaves.

Grandma joined us in the backyard and said, "Girls, now you can gather up all these limbs and dead vines from the garden and carry them over to my brush pile. And get all those limbs from my willow tree."

The willow tree reminded me of good times, playing Monopoly or Rummy with Lana at a card table, drinking Grandma's homemade lemonade. It was like a shady room under there because Grandma insisted the limbs be allowed to hang down to the ground untrimmed. Dad said the tree made a mess, all the tiny branches littering the yard. Now we could see what he meant.

We carried things all afternoon. Finally we stood by the brush pile as Grandma lit a match and held it to the willow branches. I watched the sparks fly upward into the darkness and noticed that the first stars were coming out.

"Where's Aunt Rita?" I asked.

"She went on home to fix supper, but your dad will take you girls home. He's almost finished with the storm windows."

"That reminds me." She sounded excited. "I told your dad but forgot to tell you. The McCools will be here for Thanksgiving."

"The Danny McCool you told me about?"

"Yes, I got a postcard from them today. They said they'll be having their Thanksgiving in Indianapolis with some of her relatives on Friday, and they want to stop here on the way down. I put a card in the mail saying we'd love them to stop by. It's been thirty years. Almost exactly."

"Who are the McCools?" asked Lana.

"Danny McCool is this war hero that landed his plane in one of these fields. Thirty years ago. Grandma showed me his picture." I turned to Grandma. "Which field was it, Grandma?"

She pointed toward the red barn behind us.

"Why, he flew right over the barn and landed in the cornfield over there."

"My mom never told me," said Lydia.

"Well, your mom was only six or seven at the time."

"Grandma just told me about him a few weeks ago," I said. "Danny McCool flew planes in World War II."

I turned back to Grandma. "Is he flying his plane down?"

"I suppose he'll just be driving down, Judy."

"I still want to ask him what it was like, flying those fighter planes, and what Europe was like."

"It was war, kiddo. Not like taking a vacation. You've seen Vietnam on TV. War is just horrible."

"World War II was different, I heard people say it was different, it was a good war. And Danny McCool was in Europe, which is different from Vietnam."

Grandma was quiet. We all sat quietly looking at the fire.

"I'm not always going to live around here," I said. "I want to see the world. I've never even been out of the state."

"Your Grandpa and I lived in Lafayette for a while when we were first married," Grandma said. "We didn't like it, though."

"I mean far away. I might live in California when I grow up, or Maine."

"So you want to belong to the 'jet set'?"

"What's that?"

"It's these people nowadays that just fly everywhere and move all the time."

"Yes, I want to be in the jet set."

I looked up into the sky, where more and more stars appeared, like little lights turning on. People who say stars look like diamonds on a velvet cloth are wrong. I saw depth, endless black depth, filled with uncountable suns. It was like I could fall into that depth if it wasn't for gravity holding me on earth. We all lifted our faces to the sky, as if we could see into the future.

"Hey, look at the moon," Lana said, pointing behind me to the nearly full moon rising in the east. I turned around and looked at its bright face. It seemed I could picture a jolly man looking down at me. I could see the man in the moon.

"Do you think we'll ever make it to the moon, Grandma?" I asked.

"Why should we?" asked Lana.

"I guess we'll surely try," said Grandma, "like mountain climbers who climb mountains just because they're there."

"Yes, just because it's there," I agreed, looking straight at the moon.

And then Grandma said the most amazing thing. "Did I tell you that Danny McCool works for NASA? At the Manned Spacecraft Center in Houston."

My mouth fell open. NASA. The space program. Maybe Danny McCool was working on the flight to the moon.

CHAPTER 11

October 1938
Friday and Saturday

T HE WIND BLEW STRONG ON FRIDAY MORNING, FOLLOWED BY A steady rain that settled in after morning milking. Danny sat with the Walstra family around the kitchen table eating the last of their eggs and bread. The girls stood up and carried their dishes to the sink.

"We might as well go to town now," Russ said to Danny. "Get the rest of those things Devore needs to fix the plane. Seems he ran into some problems with the landing struts. Sooner we get it fixed, the sooner you can get on with your life."

Rita and Ellen stood by the door, ready for school. "Does Danny have to leave so soon? Can't he stay longer?"

"He's not on a holiday, girls," said Mary. "Here comes the hack."

Danny lifted his hand in a salute. "Best to obey the commanding officer," he said.

The girls raised their hands to their foreheads in like manner and then rushed giggling out the door.

Russ and Danny drove into town and parked in front of the J.D. Allman store.

"Still here, Mr. McCool?" Mr. Allman said, as they walked through the door.

The man couldn't help himself, apparently, from glancing down at Danny's white shoes. Danny walked up to the counter and put his right hand down, looking straight at Mr. Allman. "Looks like you're still here and so am I." Danny smiled, but Mr. Allman turned away and looked to Russ.

"We're having trouble getting those struts stabilized," Russ said. He handed Mr. Allman a list Devore had made for him. Again they searched the aisles of the store and soon had a pile of items on the counter to be tallied up.

Russ laid a box of shotgun shells off to the side. "I need these for myself. Got a fox after the chickens." They paid for their purchases and walked outside. Danny set the box of supplies in the car.

"I'd like to get some gifts for Mary and the girls, if you don't mind," he said. "So they can remember this crazy aviator. And just to say thank you."

"That ain't necessary," Russ said. "We got work to do, see. Time's a wasting."

Danny insisted. "It won't take long."

They crossed the street to the Model Cash Store, which advertised, "Clothing, Shoes, & Furnishings." Below the sign, a deep display window contained suits, dresses, and hats for men and women. The store was narrow but extended far to the rear, lined on both sides with shelves. Danny and Russ walked past boxes of shoes on the left and display cases of gloves and hats on the right. Danny selected a navy hat with a small feather for Mary. He picked up a pair of tan leather gloves and tossed them to Russell.

"Try these on," he said.

Russ pulled on the gloves and clenched his fists several times.

"How do they feel?" Danny asked.

"I really don't think you should get me anything," Russ said, taking the gloves off and handing them back to Danny.

"It's the least I can do." He pressed the gloves into Russ's hand and started walking away. "Say, what do we have back here?" Danny continued toward the back of the store, where luggage and other specialty items were kept.

He scanned the shelves containing imported dolls in brightly colored print dresses next to a row of shiny varnished music boxes. He turned to the owner's wife, who had trailed them to the back. "I would like two of those dolls, please." The woman took the dolls off the shelf and cradled them in her hands.

"The heads, arms, and legs are made of porcelain," she said, lifting the skirts to expose the white legs. "The faces are hand painted. Very nice."

"Now see, those are expensive. You don't need to do that," Russ said.

"No, I want them for the girls."

They left the store with three brown parcels, wrapped and tied with string, and a new pair of tan leather gloves, which Russ laid on the dashboard of the car.

Friday night after supper and chores, the family moved into the sitting room. The girls sat on the floor listening to *The Green Hornet* on the radio; Mary poured the pieces of a jigsaw puzzle onto a walnut side table. Danny left the room and returned with the wrapped parcels he had hidden under his daybed. He presented the gifts with a flourish and a bow. Ellen and Rita opened the packages and held the dolls gently, rubbing their hands over the smooth china faces and the fine fabric. Rita walked up to Danny and hugged him.

"I love you, Mr. McCool."

Ellen stood nearby and held the doll to her chest.

"Thank you. It's beautiful," she said.

Mary gasped at the delicate hat, took it out of its box, placed it on her head, and then turned from side to side, face beaming.

"How do I look?" she asked Russ.

Russell stood up. "Well, I might as well show you my new gloves." He walked slowly into the kitchen while Mary took off her hat and rubbed the feather next to her cheek. When Russell returned, he placed the gloves in Mary's hands. She looked straight at Russell as she said, "Thank you, Danny. This means a lot to us."

By noon on Saturday, the work on the plane was finished. It was unseasonably warm, a beautiful autumn day. Danny stood back to examine the Fairchild 24, which stood sturdy and straight in the field. Using the new materials, he and Devore had spent Saturday morning leveling the bent wing and repairing the landing gear as best they could.

"All we need now is the fuel," Devore said. "I can get some at the airport in Lafayette."

They sat on the grass watching young Robert James as he walked around the plane, running his hand along the side of the wing.

Danny noticed Robert's gaze turn back across the field where Ellen walked toward them in black boots, her long coat trailing over the tall grass. She carried a blue bowl of apples. Robert, sleeves rolled up over his young muscles, accepted an apple from her hand and then opened the engine compartment to show her what he'd learned about the Fairchild 24 engine. She listened as if airplanes were her favorite subject. Danny and Devore watched from where they sat on the ground nearby. Robert walked to the side of the plane and rolled the cabin windows up and down.

"Look at this. Just like a car window, and this door handle, just like a '35 Plymouth."

The men smiled at each other.

Danny took up the Hoagland brothers' offer to meet them for a card game. Dressed in white shirt, gray pants, and leather jacket, he made the trip to town in Russell's car, parked near Shooter's Bar, and walked inside. A Remington rifle hung behind the counter, a nod to the name of the bar and the name of the town. Otherwise it looked like any other bar, shelves lined with various-shaped bottles, a few customers leaning heavily on the counter, a potbellied stove near a handful of tables.

As Danny stood just inside the door, Harold came forward and greeted him with a slap on the back. He led him by the arm around the counter to a back room filled with cigarette smoke, where he introduced him to Big Mike, who was tall as well as big, and Ray, who looked more like a scholar than a farmer, round rimless glasses set midway down his nose. The men made room for him in a wooden booth that looked like it was built for giants.

"They tell me you're the aviator," Big Mike said. His wool shirt-sleeves ended well above his wrists as he reached across the table to shake Danny's hand.

"That's right and all the drinks are on me," Danny announced. "Do you have Old Manhattan?"

"Never heard of it."

Danny looked at the Falstaff advertisement on the wall behind Big Mike. "Then bring us Falstaff."

"Okay, let's see what you've got, Danny McCool." Herb shuffled the cards and dealt them out. The waitress brought a tray of beers for all. The games went on until late that night.

CHAPTER 12

October 1968

Dad was not thrilled about Danny McCool and his wife coming for Thanksgiving. I overheard him talking on the phone with Grandma.

"It just seems strange to me. We don't know his wife, and I haven't seen him for thirty years. Why should he be at our family Thanksgiving dinner?"

There was a period of silence before Dad said, "I guess so. I was just never that comfortable with him myself."

"Sure I'll be cordial."

Later that morning Grandma stopped by with a sack of apples from her orchard. I asked her about what I'd overheard.

"Your father probably got his low opinion of Danny McCool from talking to your grandpa Walstra. He was always so suspicious of him." She frowned and shook her head. "But Danny stayed with us for over a week and was so helpful and such a gentleman. He came from the city. I thought he was like a breath of fresh air to us."

She placed the red apples in a glass bowl. "He just had some growing up to do. I will be glad to see him again." She stared out the kitchen window. "And Mr. Devore the mechanic, he didn't think much of Danny either, but you know the Devores, how they like to gossip. I think we should show hospitality, especially on Thanksgiving. Right, kiddo?" She pushed the bowl across the table toward me. "Have an apple."

"You're right." I took one of the apples out of the bowl. "I want to see Danny McCool, too."

Lana always stayed overnight for Halloween, which fell on a Thursday this year. We walked home after school past a house with sheets hanging from tree limbs like ghosts and another house with a cardboard skeleton dancing in the front window. We were still at odds about our friends, but we came to a truce by the time we reached my porch. We decided that I would sit with Kristy's little group at lunch and she would sit with Lydia and we just left it at that. We were still family and that wouldn't change.

Mom and Aunt Rita had never cared for Halloween. They didn't like little kids dressing up as ghosts and witches, so they were glad the Methodist church offered a party of its own. We were happy because we could still dress up and get candy. Dad didn't care one way or the other, but he always supported what Mom had wanted. She had been serious about her beliefs; I knew she was in heaven.

Marty left after supper with his friends Eddie, Nick, and Brad Wilson. He could do whatever he wanted, it seemed. Dad even let him take our truck again. Lana and I went upstairs to get ready. The summer Olympics in Mexico City had been on TV for the past two weeks, which inspired Lana to dress as a gymnast. She zipped up the jacket of a blue warm-up suit with matching pants, pulled her hair back into a ponytail, and hung a gold medal around her neck. I cut zigzags around the bottom of some old jeans and dressed as a pirate, complete with eye patch, bandana, and a quite realistic cardboard sword.

Aunt Rita drove us to the church. The twins went with us this year, dressed up as Crayola crayons. They could barely walk in the narrow tubes painted red and blue, their arms sticking out the sides for balance, pointed cones tilting on their heads. Aunt Rita said it wasn't her best idea because the boys kept falling over.

Lydia didn't come, even though Lana asked her, and I didn't even invite Kristy. I knew she'd be out trick-or-treating.

We were back home by nine o'clock. We changed into pajamas and went up to the attic. I opened the window. It was warm for October, but the wind had picked up, knocking over trash cans and rattling the dry oak leaves. Clouds moved as if caught up in a swift river.

"It looks just like Halloween," Lana said.

"Well, it is Halloween, silly."

We watched the few remaining parents and kids who were moving from lighted porch to lighted porch, holding out paper sacks for candy. One mother dressed like a witch held the hand of a little boy with a fake ax sticking out of his head.

"I can see why Mom doesn't like Halloween," Lana said.

"Well, at least we have some candy." I opened my sack and dumped it all onto the trunk and then sorted it into piles. I chose a jawbreaker since I'd already eaten a bag of malted milk balls and a Slo Poke sucker. I put the rest back in the sack.

"What now?" I said. I felt stirred up, like I was missing something.

We followed the winding path around furniture and boxes to the other end of the attic and looked out the south window. The backdoor light bulb cast a faint gleam over the yard. The clothesline flapped in the wind. Now and then the waning moon shone like a pale wafer between the clouds. The moon looked ominous. Tree branches twisted about in the wind. The old glass in the windows shook. I was beginning to feel chilly and a little melancholy.

"Let's go back downstairs," I said. I turned out the light, and we felt our way down the stairs.

The explorers traveled down the dark tunnel toward the center of the pyramid. Their lamps had burned out. They felt their way along, hands on the cold walls, afraid to turn back, afraid to go on. Suddenly they saw the rectangle of a door ahead, faintly outlined in white. There must be light beyond the door. But how? What could it be?

I opened the door to my bedroom. We passed through to the hall and down the stairs to the living room, where everything was cozy and warm. Dad sat in his brown chair watching the end of *Dragnet*.

When we reached the kitchen, I had an idea. I turned to Lana. "I dare us to sneak out of the house tonight. Like at Kristy's party."

"It's a school night."

"I don't care. It will give us something to do for Halloween."

"I don't think we should."

"Don't be such a Goody Two-shoes."

She hated when I called her that. "Okay," she said.

I opened a box of Ritz crackers, and we joined Dad in the living room to watch *The Dean Martin Show*. By ten thirty he said we needed to go to bed because of school so we said good night and went upstairs. We waited until eleven thirty to make sure Dad was asleep before we made our move. By that time I think Lana was finally coming around to my side, or at least wasn't as reluctant. I put a sweatshirt over my pajamas.

"Aren't we getting dressed?"

"No, we have to wear pajamas. That's the way Kristy does it."

Lana rolled her eyes.

The house had been quiet for a long time, so we left the room and crept down the stairs, hesitating at every creak of the wood. We refused to giggle or laugh. We reached the bottom of the stairs and tiptoed down the hall to the back door.

"Girls, are you still up?" It was Dad, calling from his downstairs bedroom. "Yeah, we just needed a drink of milk."

"Since when do you drink milk at night?"

"Lana wanted it," I said.

She glared at me. We got a glass of milk and went back upstairs.

"Don't tell Kristy," I said. I didn't want her to know we couldn't pull it off.

"No problem," said Lana. "She's not my friend."

When we woke the next morning, it was much colder and the streets were wet from rain. The furnace had turned on overnight.

Dad said, "I think our nice weather is over. Get ready for snow one of these days."

I looked out the window. The wind had blown away most of the remaining leaves from the maple trees. The oak leaves were still hanging on. It was a gray and brown world outside.

"You'll need your coats," Dad said.

"I brought mine," Lana said, "pulling it out of her overnight bag. "Mom watched the weather last night and knew it was going to cool off."

"Where's mine?" I asked Dad.

"I don't know. Try the closet or maybe it's in a box somewhere." Mom always took care of that kind of thing. Now we had to search for what we needed. I opened the closet door and pushed aside Marty's and Dad's coats looking for mine. I found my coat on the closet floor in a wad. I shook it in the air and then pulled it on as we rushed out the front door.

My bare legs were cold as we walked down the sidewalk as fast as we could. "I should have put on knee socks," I said.

Mr. Kaminsky stood by his porch steps, pounding a wooden cutout of a turkey into the ground. He looked up at us. We said hi, but he didn't chat with us this time. I knew how he felt.

Mom used to complain every year about their million decorations. "How can they afford all those lights at Christmas with their four kids? Do they really think it looks attractive?"

"It's a free country, Ellen," was always Dad's answer.

Now I just felt sorry for them with Steven gone. I would never criticize their decorations again.

After Halloween, our class at school started to get ready for the Thanksgiving play. As sixth-graders we had the main parts and the most responsibility. I signed up to help paint the backdrop. This meant I stayed after school, brought along a sandwich to eat, and changed into Marty's old sweatpants and flannel shirt. Since we kids thought it was funny to swipe a little paint on someone's arm or back, my own shirt was soon crisscrossed with brown brushstrokes. Mrs. Clark, in blue jeans rolled up at the cuffs, was there to supervise, but she had a hard time keeping us on task. I had never seen her without a dress and pearls.

We painted brown tree trunks with black highlights following the chalk outlines drawn by the art teacher, Mr. Sweeney. Then we painted dark green evergreens, using short slashing motions of the brush, and used large swirling strokes of yellow and orange for autumn foliage. Randy was one of the boys on the painting committee, so I stood next to him whenever possible.

We quit early on the third day of painting. Mrs. Clark had had enough, though she did say we were doing a fine job. "I believe it is truly beginning to look like a forest," she said, standing at the back of the room, hands on hips, her big white shirt amazingly clean.

Randy had to wait for his dad to pick him up, so I stood outside with him near the bike racks in front of the school. "You've got paint on your face," I said.

"So do you." He pointed toward the top of my head. "You've got some in your hair, too."

I reached up to my bangs and felt a strand of hair that was stuck together. I laughed.

He opened his gym bag. "I've got a candy bar. You want some?"

"Sure, I'm starving."

He pulled the wrapper off the Snickers bar, broke it in half, and offered me a piece.

We sat down on the curb and ate in silence. An orange light flickered through the trees at the edge of the schoolyard. I thought it was a streetlight, but then I realized it was the moon. "Look, Randy." I pointed toward the east.

We watched as the perfectly full moon slowly inched higher and cleared the trees. It hung there like an orange balloon.

"Wow," Randy said. "It looks bigger than normal."

I somehow knew it wasn't the time to give a scientific explanation of why it looked bigger near the horizon and why it was orange and why it was called the harvest moon.

"I know. It's beautiful." It was like we were in a spell for several minutes.

Randy broke the spell. "It's getting dark. When I get home I've still got to do chores. I feed and water the pigs and calves."

"I have to fix supper, unless Dad fixed something already."

"You waiting on a ride?" he asked.

"No, my bike's right here." He realized now I wasn't waiting on a ride, I was just staying to be with him. I might have turned a little pink, but he just smiled. It was an encouraging sign.

Things were going along fine, and then Lydia hit Kristy in the head playing dodge ball. It was during late afternoon Phys. Ed. I watched from the sidelines after being hit in the leg by Priscilla, the tallest girl in the class, stronger than most of the boys. She and Lydia were the only ones left on their side, Kristy and two other girls were left on our side. I wasn't paying too much attention until a ball smashed Kristy's head against the wall and she sat right down on the floor. I turned toward the other end of the gym to Priscilla, but it was Lydia stepping back from the throw. She had her arms raised as if to say, "Oops, I didn't mean to hit her." But I know Lydia. If she can hit a target with a gun, she can aim and hit someone's head, so I didn't think it was an accident.

The game stopped as everyone stared at Kristy, blood running from her nose. Several of the girls gathered 'round as the teacher gave her a wad of Kleenex and helped her stand up. A pink spot covered her right cheek. As they walked out of the gym past Lydia, Kristy managed to squeak out, "Are you stupid? Why'd you do that?"

"It was an accident," Lydia said. "I meant to throw it lower." But she didn't look that sorry and made no move to join the others.

Lana walked over to me and said, "Kristy should have been paying attention. She just talks instead of playing the game."

I turned on her. "You know Lydia. She aimed right for her head. She knew what she was doing."

"You don't know that."

"She and Priscilla act like this is some championship game or something. It's just Phys. Ed."

Lana left me and walked over to Lydia, who stood alone. Most of the kids seemed to agree with me. Stephanie said to me, "What a cheap shot." The teacher returned and told us all to go back to our classroom.

Kristy missed one day of school, but she was fine. Her nose was not broken. She came back to school with a black eye, which only seemed to attract more attention to her than ever. I hated the way Lana defended Lydia all the time, even when she was clearly wrong.

CHAPTER 13

October 1938
Sunday

Sunday morning Mary clicked down the stairs in sturdy-heeled shoes, black dress belted at the waist, hair arranged in waves. She entered the kitchen, where Danny McCool, true to his word, stood by the table in freshly pressed white shirt and blue checked tie. He had promised Ellen and Rita he would go to church with them, and he was ready, even after helping Russ early with the milking.

"Do you go to church often in Chicago?" Mary asked.

"Oh, I've been there," Danny said. "Beautiful churches in Chicago, beautiful majestic architecture. Always feel better when I go. I intend to go more. It's the right thing to do, of course."

The girls soon joined them and they walked out to the Model A, which Russell had pulled up close to the house. Danny walked Mary around the car, opened the door, and held her hand as she stepped inside. She scooted over by Russell and said, "I feel like a queen being escorted to the ball. See how he opened the door for me?"

Russell pulled on his new pair of gloves and offered no comment. Danny helped the girls into the back of the car and sat down beside them. He tapped Russell on the shoulder. "All ready back here."

They drove the two miles to the Methodist church, which sat solidly in the center of Remington as if the town had been built around it. It looked as if it was built to last forever. As they walked through the vestibule and into the sanctuary, Mary observed how Danny shook hands and chatted with people in the congregation, the girls always at his side. He introduced himself to Pastor Birch with a vigorous handshake and then chatted with people all around. She considered how easy it was for him to talk to people, so unlike their German and Dutch neighbors.

After dinner and the evening milking, the family gathered in the sitting room. Mary sat in a wing chair next to Danny, who sat on the floor and leaned his head against the Philco radio, twisting the knob.

"Here it is, *The Eddie Cantor Show.*"

Violin music from David Rubinoff drifted from the little radio. Russ sat in his chair, shotgun between his knees, Hoppe's cleaning fluid open on the table beside him. The familiar sharp scent filled the room as he cleaned the barrel and wiped down the wood. Danny rose from the floor, then sat down on the davenport between Ellen and Rita, stretching his arms out like wings behind their heads.

"This is swell, ain't it, girls?"

No one spoke. The violin music rose and fell.

Russ finished his cleaning and set the gun aside. "Ellen," he said. "Go get your mother's clarinet." Ellen got up and shortly returned with a black leather case, which she unclasped and opened flat on the floor. She removed the clarinet parts, put them together, and adjusted the reed. She handed it to her mother. Mary stood in the middle of the room, smiled at each person in her little audience, and then played along with the melody coming from the radio, at times adding parts of her own. Everyone clapped when the song was finished, and she bowed deeply before them. She handed the clarinet to Ellen and sat back down in the chair.

"Now it's your turn, Ellen," she said. "Show them what you've learned."

Ellen put the clarinet to her mouth, waiting for the next song on the radio. She smiled at Danny, who nodded his head in encouragement. When the song started she shut her eyes and played long simple notes, clear and smooth.

Mary leaned back, resting her head against the back of the chair.

"I do thank you for the battery, Danny. I didn't realize how much we missed the radio." She closed her eyes. "It is a treat."

CHAPTER 14

Fall 1968

With Kristy it was always a surprise. I never knew what she was going to do next. She called me on a Tuesday right after school. "Meet me at the Caboose, okay?"

I dropped everything to change clothes and look in the mirror. I patted some water on my hair to get it in shape and hurried downtown.

I slid into a booth seat across from Kristy. The bruise around her eye was completely gone. Rhonda came soon afterward and sat beside her. The waitress who walked toward us was Caroline Mayhugh, Lydia's mom. It looked like she was trying to hide her weariness with color, blue shadow above her eyes and pink frost on her lips. She took a pencil out of her checkered apron.

"Hey, Judy." Her eyes brightened when she saw me, one of the few faces she knew in town. Apparently she didn't know that Lydia and I were not such friends anymore. "Can I take y'all's order?"

I saw Kristy and Rhonda snicker across the table.

"Hi, Caroline," I said. "Lyd told me you worked here." I looked away. Kristy said, "So, bring us three chocolate shakes. It's on me."

As Caroline walked away, Rhonda mimicked, "Y'all. Can I take y'all's order?" She turned to me. "They live in that church, don't they?"

"Yeah, they said it's not so bad." I rearranged my silverware.

"I guess you could say they have to go to church every day," Kristy said. She and Rhonda laughed like it was the funniest thing ever. I laughed along with them but felt a little bad about it.

"I'm getting new furniture for my bedroom," Rhonda said. "All white."

"That's neat. We're going shopping, too," Kristy added, "down in Lafayette. There's no place around here to shop. I need new clothes."

I had nothing to say about that.

Caroline finally brought the shakes and set them on the table.

Kristy pulled a straw from its wrapper and stuck it in her shake. "Have you ever gone steady, Jude?" she asked.

"I'd go steady with Randy if he wanted to," I said, stirring my shake with the straw like Kristy did. "We're good friends. We hang out."

"Which one's Randy?" she asked.

"The boy at the end of your row with the dark hair, long in front."

"Always wears cowboy boots," Rhonda added.

"Oh." She looked like she was trying to place him.

I didn't mention that I had never had a real boyfriend or that Dad said I was too young to go steady.

"How 'bout you guys?" I asked.

Rhonda spoke up. "I've been going with Rick since summer."

"I'm just playing the field right now," Kristy said. "I had to break up with my boyfriend when we moved here."

"Yeah, I guess I'm playing the field, too," I said.

"What about your brother, Marty?"

"What about him?"

"Is he available?" Kristy asked.

"Well, he's pretty busy with basketball." I took a big gulp of my shake and then added, "You know he's over sixteen years old." My forehead hurt from swallowing the cold drink so fast.

"So what?"

"Nothing. He's nothing special. His room stinks."

"I think he's cute," Kristy said. She pulled a wad of napkins from the dispenser and wiped her mouth. "Hey, does your dad drink?" Kristy asked.

"Sure, all the time, usually iced tea."

Rhonda and Kristy looked at each other, and Rhonda laughed.

"You're so naïve," Kristy said. "It's cute."

I felt myself sweating as I tried to keep up with the conversation. "He does drink beer," I said. I had seen Dad drink a beer now and then after Mom died. I felt as though I were under interrogation. I couldn't afford to say anything else stupid.

"Hey, Jude. It's okay," Kristy said, tapping her fingernails on the table.

Maybe I didn't fit in. I didn't say the right things.

Kristy stood up. "When are you going to invite me to your house, Jude?"

"Uh, soon."

"Friday?"

My head was spinning. I needed some time to get our house in shape. I needed to clean my bedroom and the whole house, actually. I was worried what she'd think about all the cars in our front yard and our worn-out furniture.

"Sure, I'll talk to Dad. You know where I live, don't you?" I asked. "Your brother's been there with Marty."

"I don't have a brother."

I looked at her and wondered what she was trying to prove. "Brad?"

"Brad's my uncle."

I must be an idiot. Nothing made sense.

"He's my dad's little brother." She looked at me like I should have known.

"Why didn't you tell me?"

"I never said he was my brother."

"You didn't say anything."

I was irritated but let it go.

Back home, the kitchen was humid from something boiling on the stove. Dad was actually making supper tonight. He was reading the instructions on a Kraft macaroni and cheese box. I could see the black grease in the creases of his hands and under his fingernails. His hands never looked clean. He saw my look.

"I washed my hands. They're just stained." He took a small box out of the freezer. "Where you been?"

"Down at the Caboose with Kristy. Can she come over on Friday?"

"Okay with me. You might want to straighten up a few things around the house." He dropped a perfect square of frozen broccoli into a saucepan with a clunk. "I'm making a good, well-balanced meal tonight, Blue Jay."

The frozen broccoli reminded me of something. "Mrs. Clark told us about microwave ovens today. She has one and so does Kristy's mom."

"What do they use them for?" He turned on the gas burner under the pan.

"To heat food up. That broccoli would be cooked in just a few minutes."

"Really?"

"Yeah, it saves her time and she can heat up leftovers in a plastic dish."

Dad stood still. "Your mom wouldn't have wanted one. She would say we don't need to pay hundreds of dollars for something we don't need." He turned down the heat on the stove and looked back at me. "But maybe we'll get one anyway when work picks up."

"When's that going to happen?" I said softly.

"What?"

"Nothing."

"What about your chores? I think it's time you did the laundry, Jude. I'm out of work pants."

I picked up a plastic basket from the bathroom and started with Marty's room upstairs. His gym bag with sweaty basketball clothes sat plump and zipped shut on the floor. I picked up the whole bag and threw it out in the hallway. I would empty the bag into the washer without touching anything.

Marty paid no attention to me from where he sat in bed looking at a *Sports Illustrated* magazine.

I stuck my foot under the bed to kick out some blue jeans I saw there and felt something sharp. I pulled out the jeans and saw the edge of a sheet of red metal.

"What's this?"

Marty looked up. "Hey, get out of my room!"

"Dad said I had to do the laundry. What is this thing?"

I pulled on the heavy metal. "It looks like a stop sign!"

"It is, you idiot." He stood up from the bed and shut the door.

"But why do you have a stop sign in your room?"

"It's not mine. It's Brad's. Well, it's not his, but it's a long story. We're storing it here. And you better not say anything about it to Dad. Or anybody else."

"Who's we?"

"Nick and Brad and Eddie. It was Brad's idea. But I don't need to tell you anything. Get out."

"Did you know Brad isn't Kristy's brother?"

"Sure, he's her uncle." So I was the only one who didn't know.

"Did you guys steal that sign?"

"No. You can't steal something that doesn't belong to anybody."

"It belongs to someone…like the government. It's probably against the law."

Marty seemed to be thinking.

"Hey, I didn't do it." He paused, still thinking. "We sell these signs to college students in Renssalaer, at St. Joseph's College. It was Brad's idea. He's done it before. Those college kids hang them up in their dorm rooms."

"So why are they here? In your room?"

"We used Dad's truck one day and something came up and we had to hide them real quick. So don't make a federal case out of it."

"You mean, there's more?"

"Yes…I mean, no. I mean it's none of your business. Don't worry about it. I'll get rid of them."

"Can I help you?" It was beginning to sound like an adventure. Something Kristy would do.

"No. And don't tell anybody." His look was so cold it scared me a little.

"I won't. But I still want to help you."

"No."

It took two trips to get all the clothes, sheets, and towels down to the washer and dryer in the basement. I dumped everything out and began sorting into piles according to color and dirtiness. I looked over toward Dad's workbench and the robot. Marty and Dad spent weeks building that robot before Mom died. But then they stopped, and now Marty wasn't interested in things like that. The robot stood in the corner, a boxy metal figure on four wheels with two round eyes and a straight-line mouth. It could roll forward powered by a lawn-mower motor, but it couldn't do anything else even though dials and buttons covered its chest. It reminded me of the Jetsons' robot without arms.

That would look nice in my room, I thought. *Something different and unusual. Kristy would like it.*

Thursday morning Marty rushed into the kitchen, where I sat with Dad eating Cheerios.

"Don't forget my first basketball game next Saturday, the 23rd. It's a home game and I'm starting."

Dad said, "I'll be there. Don't you want something to eat?"

Marty grabbed a handful of Cheerios out of the open box. "The coach is taking us out for breakfast. Gotta go."

I followed Marty out the front door and grabbed his arm.

"I've been thinking about those signs," I said.

"Will you stay out of it? Geez." He pulled his arm away.

"Can I have your robot?"

"No." He walked down the front steps.

"It might keep me from telling about the signs."

He stopped and turned around. "Take the robot, then. I don't care about that junk anymore."

After school I went to the basement to get the robot. It was heavier than I thought, but I managed to carry it up two sets of stairs to my room. I put it right at the foot of my bed and then stood back for a look. Nothing was coordinated in my room like in Kristy's. My bedspread looked like a patchwork quilt, but it wasn't really a quilt. It was bought on sale at Penney's. Years ago. A poster of the Beatles hung next to my map of the United States on walls painted the color of celery. The only thing I had ever collected was books. Old books from the library, birthday present books, paperbacks from school. I had outgrown my one doll and stuffed animals. I thought the robot added a lot to the room.

Downstairs I dusted the end tables and knickknacks and vacuumed the floor, but I couldn't do anything about the cars in the driveway or the junk around the garage. This was as good as it was going to get. Dad picked up some frozen pizzas and Cokes at the grocery store, we had some chips, so there was nothing else to do.

Friday about five o'clock the Wilsons' red Oldsmobile stopped in front of the house, and I watched Kristy walk to the door carrying a little blue suitcase. I let her in before she knocked. She didn't ask any questions about the used cars so I was relieved.

"Where's everybody else?" she asked, looking around the empty living room.

"Dad's in the kitchen, and Marty's still at practice."

"Oh. Well, show me around."

"Want something to eat?"

"Sure."

I took Kristy to the kitchen. I had the pizza on the counter, ready for the oven.

Dad turned around from the refrigerator with Cokes in his hands. "Hi, Kristy. Hi, Blue Jay. These are nice and chilled for you girls." He took a Coke for himself and walked toward the living room. "Bring me a couple pieces of pizza when it's ready."

"Your dad seems nice," Kristy said. She pointed to a stack of library books on the kitchen table. "You read a lot, don't you?"

"Yeah, I like mysteries the best."

"Sometimes I pick up magazines at the library for Mom, or a book for my dad. He's a lawyer."

"I know." I put the pizza in the oven and set the timer. We went upstairs. Kristy stopped in the doorway to my room.

"Wow, what's that?"

Apparently the robot did make a good first impression.

"It's a robot. Marty made it."

She giggled and turned to the rest of the room, running her eyes over the walls, forming her opinions. "I like your posters."

She walked up to the robot and placed her hands at each side of its head to lift it up. "It's heavy."

"I know. I had to carry it up from the basement." After a short pause I said, "We call it Buster." I made the name up on the spot.

"What's it do?"

"Oh, it just lights up." I turned it on.

"Neat," she said. She walked over to the telescope that I had placed at an angle in front of the window.

"Well, what do you want to do?" I asked.

"What is there?"

"We could watch TV." I should have had better plans. "Or sneak out later."

She pulled the eyepiece of the telescope toward her without loosening the knobs.

"Watch out, don't break it."

"Okay, okay." She stepped back. "Gee!"

"Sorry, let me show you." I twisted it around, opened the window, and poked the scope outside. "Here."

I sighted in the flag at the top of the elevator and showed it to Kristy. "See, you can see all the detail in the flag and the birds on the roof."

Kristy squinted through the eyepiece. "Yeah."

"Wait, I've got a better idea. I just discovered this last week."

I folded up the legs of the telescope and started up the stairs with Kristy following. The telescope was awkward to carry and kept banging into the wall. At the top of the stairs, I led the way to the east end, where I opened the window and set up the telescope. We were surrounded with dusty boxes and pink insulation.

"It's dirty up here," Kristy said. She wiped bits of insulation off her pants. "Why do we have to come up here, anyway?"

I had to get her interested quickly. "Let me show you what we can see from up here. From the north window over there, we can see the elevator and the water tower. I can actually see your backyard from this window when the leaves are all gone like this."

"You spying on us? That's creepy." Lines formed between her eyebrows.

"No. Of course not. I never saw anything. It's just your backyard furniture." I trained the telescope to see through a small space between tree limbs to the patio table in Kristy's yard.

"Hey, your mom's out there tonight. She doesn't even have a coat on."

"Let me see," Kristy said. She shoved me aside and looked through the eyepiece. "Let's don't do this. Let's go back downstairs." She stepped back and gave the scope a little shove.

I moved it back in place and looked again. Kristy's father was leaning over her mother now. Looked like they were either laughing or yelling. He was trying to get her up out of the chair.

"Let's go. I mean it." Kristy was insistent now.

"Okay, what's wrong?"

Kristy had walked back between the boxes and stood at the top of the stairs. This had been a bad idea. I left the telescope and followed her down to the bedroom.

"What now?" Kristy said. She sat down on the bed, shoulders slumped forward.

"I don't know. You want to watch TV?"

"Do you really like living out here in the country?"

"We don't live in the country."

"Believe me, Jude, this whole town is country." She swung her arm through the air.

"Yeah? Well, I don't want to stay in this old country town myself. I have plans to see the world, maybe fly planes."

Kristy stood up. She picked up one of my Hardy Boy books and laid it back down. "I just want to marry someone rich and not have to work. Maybe live by the ocean," she said. She walked to the door and looked out into the hall.

"Do you like to travel?" I asked.

"It's okay. I've been to Florida and everyplace in between."

"Do you like to fly?"

"Never have."

"Me, either. But we're going to meet a pilot next week. He works at NASA and he's a war hero from World War II. He's coming to my grandma's house. He actually stayed at their house when Mom was a little girl."

"That's nice." Kristy sat at my desk and started flipping through the pages of my magazines.

Sometimes I just did not know how to talk to Kristy. And her mood changed so much. I wished I would have invited someone else over, too, sort of a third party as a cushion between us.

"When do we eat?" she asked, looking up at me.

"Oh, the pizza. I forgot." We hurried downstairs.

In the kitchen, Dad was taking the pizza out of the oven while the timer buzzed away. I pushed several buttons until the timer went off.

"It's a little crispy, but it'll be okay," he said. He placed two pieces on a paper plate and returned to the living room.

I put the Cokes and a bag of potato chips in a basket with some napkins and handed it to Kristy. I put a dish towel under the cookie sheet that held the pizza because I couldn't find the pot holders, and we carried everything upstairs. We sat on the bed and began to eat. I turned on the radio to WLS Chicago and turned it up loud. "Green Tambourine" was playing. I should have turned the music on sooner because it helped me relax.

"Pizza tastes good."

"Thanks," I said, a large bite of pizza in my mouth.

"Got any ice?"

"Depends on if anybody refilled the trays. Marty never does."

This made her laugh. "I know, neither does Brad."

We started talking about school and boys. I relaxed a little more.

We had just finished eating when I heard the truck pull into the driveway. "Marty's home," I said.

Kristy jumped up. "Let's go down and see him."

We reached the bottom of the stairs just as Marty stepped through the door and threw down his bag. He looked over at Dad. "What's to eat?"

Marty ignored us even though we stood right there. We followed him into the kitchen, and he acknowledged us by saying, "Hi, Kristy." He opened one of the chilled Cokes from the refrigerator and tilted it up over his head to drink.

"Any pizza for me?"

"Sorry, we ate it all," Kristy said, smiling like a movie star.

Marty took three pieces of leftover fried chicken out of the refrigerator and poured a glass of milk. He placed the chicken on a plate next to two slices of white bread.

We stayed in the kitchen awhile longer. Kristy tried to talk to Marty, but he was focused on eating and soon joined Dad by the TV, so we went back upstairs.

Not much else happened and we went to bed. We didn't even sneak out. Kristy didn't seem as much fun at my house. Everything I'd worried about, like the trashy front yard and used cars, never came up. The only problem was just that the evening was flat. I felt like I came across as boring, and that was the last thing I wanted. Maybe she was as bored at my house as I was. Saturday morning we slept until ten, ate breakfast, and then her dad picked her up.

I wasn't good at entertaining friends. I thought of my birthday party earlier in the year, which was a disaster, even though it was a totally different situation. It was my eleventh birthday, March 10, the first birthday after Mom died, a big milestone we had to get by. Aunt Rita thought it would be good for me to have a party, to help me move on, I guess. She invited Stephanie from my class, Trudy, since she was our neighbor, and of course Lana. So, not too big, not too small. Dad, Uncle Phil, and the twins were also there. Aunt Rita made a cake like the ones you see in the *Better Homes & Gardens Cookbook*. Two layers, chocolate frosting, and eleven yellow candles on top. She decorated the kitchen with yellow and red balloons, laid out matching napkins and paper plates. Several gifts wrapped in colorful paper surrounded the cake. It was supposed to make me happy, but when they sang "Happy Birthday" and I looked again at the pile of gifts, I couldn't stop from crying. I said I was sorry but I needed to get away. I ran upstairs, shut my bedroom door, and wouldn't let anyone in, even though my friends pleaded for me to open up so we could talk.

When that didn't work, Aunt Rita came to the door. Her voice was soft and kind.

"Jude, it's normal for you to feel this way. But your friends want you to have a good birthday. We all do. Come on down and open your presents."

That made me cry louder, when she mentioned the presents. It was like something had to be let loose in me before it could get better. I think Dad understood because he never tried to talk me into coming back down.

I had ruined my own party. I fell asleep and woke up later to a dark bedroom. It was raining outside and the clock said 6:30.

I walked downstairs past the dark, silent living room into the kitchen, where the light was on. Dad sat at the table with Marty. They were eating soup and peanut butter and jelly sandwiches. The partially eaten cake was covered with Saran Wrap. My gifts were unwrapped and now sat in a row on the kitchen counter. I walked over to see what they were: a diary, a pink shirt, two necklaces, a board game called Risk, a package of different colors of knee socks, and a small record player. I picked up each gift and set it back down.

Dad didn't say anything, just went to the stove, poured a bowl of soup for me, set it on the table. I sat down on a chair. Marty pushed the loaf of bread and peanut butter jar toward me.

"Well, we made it through the first birthday," Dad said. I realized it was a first for him, too.

CHAPTER 15

October 1938
Monday

Monday was wash day. Danny remained at the table after breakfast holding the warm coffee cup in both hands. He watched Mary set a copper boiler on the stove and fill it with water. The clothes and bed linens had soaked overnight in two wooden tubs that sat near his feet, the water a dull gray.

"I'm willing to help you, Mary. I'm not sure what Russ wants me to do today."

"Then bring over that wringer," she said. "I'm sure I can find something for you to do."

She showed him how to lift the heavy linens from the tub, twist the water out, and guide them through the wringer.

"You are quite the woman," he said. "This is heavy work." He rolled up his sleeves and twisted the thick ropes of cloth.

"And rough on the hands," she added. "Thank you for the Chamberlain's lotion."

He continued the wringing while she reached for the lotion bottle. He watched her rub the lotion over her hands and arms. She didn't have the stout build of the farm women he'd shaken hands with at church. Mary's frame was delicate, but he could see the muscles in her arms. He watched her move to the stove, where she added a few sticks of wood to the fire.

The back door opened and Russ walked in. "Ready to go?" He picked up the husking gloves that lay on the table.

Mary shut the door of the stove and turned to him. "Danny's offered to help me today. There's the washing to do, and then I need to get started on the apple cider and apple butter and the girls won't be here until after school."

"Mary, we got more corn to get in today."

Danny held up his hands, as in surrender. "I'll help wherever you want, Russ. I only meant to help Mary until you got here." He dried his hands on a towel and rolled his sleeves down.

Mary stood by the stove, arms crossed. "Russell, I would appreciate some help today."

Russ poured water into a glass and took a drink. He stared at Mary in silence. "I reckon I can just do as usual." He set the glass down and walked outside.

Russ returned to the house in the early afternoon, past bed linens that unfurled in the wind like white flags. He looked through the window to see Danny standing next to Mary, a basket of apples on the floor between them. He heard Mary laugh in her quiet way that sounded like little bells. Russ opened the door, walked to the table, and took off his straw hat.

Danny turned around, apple in hand. "I'm helping make apple butter. A first time for everything." He laughed.

Russ nodded and motioned for Mary to follow him. She wiped her hands on her apron and followed him upstairs. He turned to her in the dim hallway.

"Mary, I spoke to Ray today. He stopped by the field where me and the boys were working. They tell me that Danny"—he pointed a thumb toward the kitchen—"who I guess you've taken a shine to…"

"I haven't taken a shine to Danny." She glared at Russ. "You're the one that said he could stay, and you're the one that's always saying you wished I had some help with all this work."

He swished his hand through the air as if chasing away an ir-
ritating fly.

"Mary, he took advantage of them Saturday night. Took fifteen
dollars from them playing poker."

He waited for her reaction, but there was none.

"I'm beginning to wonder about him. I'm not sure I want him
alone here with you and the girls." He looked down at his hands.
"My land, I hope we haven't made a mistake."

"You know Ray and those men," Mary said. "They'd have taken
Danny's money if they'd had the chance and thought nothing of it.
It goes both ways."

"They don't have the money like he apparently does, Mary. They
said he's involved in the liquor business. Said Danny told them so
himself. Some company in Chicago, makes Old Manhattan."

"I don't know if I believe that." She looked at Russ, confused. "He
said he flew planes for a living, at fairs. Look how he went to church
with us yesterday, so nice to everybody. And he's been a perfect gentleman to me and the girls."

"Reckon he said he also flew for Jean's father. He didn't say what
business they were in."

"He's been so helpful to me this morning," she said. "And even
before that, always ready to put dishes away and sweep the floor. And
he's so willing to help you out."

"Mary, willing ain't helping. He ain't that big of a help to me. Have
to show him every dang single step of a job and explain everything.
The sooner he leaves, the better."

They returned to the kitchen. Danny turned toward them. "Anything wrong?"

"Maybe." Russ walked toward Danny and stopped right in front
of him. "Just what kind of work do you do in Chicago anyway? Ray
says you work for a liquor company."

"That's an honest question." He leaned back against the counter.
"I work for Jean's father, who is employed by Old Manhattan. I fly a
plane for them and do work for the company. But that's not a crime.

Anyway"—he tossed his head back and snorted—"I may not have a job when I get back to Chicago. I'm not in such good favor with Mr. Swanson right now." He picked up his knife and another apple.

"What about your poker game the other night? Ray says you took them for fifteen dollars."

"We played poker. They lost." He cut the apple in half without looking up, and then without raising his voice, he waved the knife back and forth. "I bought the drinks, bought all the food. If you want to know the truth, I think they planned to cheat me." He pointed the knife toward his chest. "They thought I was an easy target. Guess they found out differently."

Russell answered, "I'm just saying, these are hardworking folks, my neighbors, see, and I better not find out you're taking advantage of them." He put his arm around Mary. "Or of us." The muscles around his mouth were tight, trembling a little.

"I give you my word," Danny said. He laid down the knife, put his hand over his heart, and then held it out toward Russell. Russ hesitated before taking his hand and shaking it one time. He turned around, picked up his hat, and walked back outside.

CHAPTER 16

Fall 1968

DAD DECIDED TO PUT UP CHRISTMAS LIGHTS ON A COLD GRAY SATurday in the middle of November. I watched him untangle the long strands of bulbs and staple them in a line along the front porch. It was cold, but we all knew the weather would get worse.

Mom had always made him wait until well after Thanksgiving to put the lights up, but he turned to me and said, "Now, Jude, I'm putting these lights up before the weather gets bad. No use climbing around up here in the cold and snow."

I handed the strings of lights up to him as he reached down from the ladder.

"We don't have to turn them on until it gets closer to Christmas. That would make your mom happy."

"Okay," I said. It made my eyes water when he talked like that.

"Now, Blue Jay, go get me that little broom to clean out these gutters."

I was glad to help Dad, unlike Marty, who was nowhere to be found.

After putting up all the Christmas lights and brushing out the gutters, we turned on the lights to see how they looked.

"Perfect," I said. The front porch was outlined in fat bulbs of many colors, and the two shrubs on either side of the steps twinkled with white lights in lacy strings. It wasn't the big display we used to have, back when we outlined the windows and strung lights through the trees, but it was better than last year, when we didn't put up any lights at all.

"They're beautiful," I said. Dad unplugged the lights and we went inside.

I found apple cider in the refrigerator and poured some into two clean plastic cups.

"Where's Marty?" Dad asked.

"I don't know. Probably with all those boys he hangs out with." I sipped at my cider. "I hope he isn't getting in trouble." I lifted one eye up toward Dad to see his reaction. Mom had always worried about Marty, about the boys he was with and what he was doing.

Dad said, "Don't worry, Jude. I used to be a teenager like him, and I turned out all right." He looked at me with a grin.

I couldn't picture Dad as a teenager.

We heard a knock at the front door and Aunt Rita called out, "Anybody home?"

"Come on in," Dad called out.

Uncle Phil entered the kitchen carrying a cardboard box with Aunt Rita, Lana, and the twins close behind. The twins went straight up to Marty's room, where he had a box of Lincoln logs and his old toy cars for them to play with.

"You girls are going to look like real Indians," Aunt Rita beamed. She was never happier than when she had finished a creative project.

Lana reached into the box and pulled out strings of colorful beads and strips of tan cloth covered with geometric patterns. "Look at the necklaces and headbands Mom made."

Aunt Rita was in charge of the Indian costumes for the Thanksgiving play at the school and as usual she had gone overboard. She held up a large library book with a picture of a somber American Indian wearing a feathered headdress on the jacket cover. She flipped through the pages until she found the picture she wanted.

"Now, you may not look like the authentic Indians of the Northeast of that time period, but I suppose the audience won't know the difference."

Phil said, "Don't be ridiculous, Rita. Nobody will know the difference." He set the box down on the table.

"You two will make beautiful Indian maidens," Dad said.

"Dad, we're going to be Indian braves," I said.

"Okay-, cute little braves," he said and winked.

There were so many girls in our class that some of us had to dress as boys, but I didn't mind being a brave instead of a squaw anyway. We had lines to say and a poem to recite to the Pilgrims.

Aunt Rita picked up two Indian vests.

"I just finished these this afternoon," she said as she held them up for us to see. The vests were tan with Indian symbols painted on the front and back and a short fringe cut around the bottom.

"I ordered some light tan tights from Sears for you girls, and we can use these dark gold hand towels for your loincloths. You'll top it off with the beads and headbands with feathers. You can just go barefoot so we don't have to buy moccasins."

"We're gonna look great. I just hope I remember my lines."

The twins came screaming down the stairs.

"Pipe down, you two," yelled Phil. "I think it's time to go, Rita."

"We've got to go deliver the rest of these to your teacher and then go buy some clothes for the twins," Rita added.

She grabbed the hands of the two boys, and they all left through the front door.

The dress rehearsal for our holiday program was scheduled for the Friday before Thanksgiving. I knew my lines, and my complete Indian outfit hung ready on a metal hanger like a clothing display in a store. That morning I took my outfit from the hanger, folded it neatly into my duffel bag, and threw the bag over my shoulder. Since my bike tire was flat, I jogged toward school, bag flapping against my back. Kids were still walking up to the doors from the buses when I got there.

The heavy rucksack flapped against the soldier's back as he approached the collection area. The orphaned children got off the trucks and entered the bombed-out school building clutching their possessions, waiting to be picked up and flown to safety. The soldier approached with gun ready. The planes were nearby. They would soon fly to safety. The soldier approached the group.

"Hey, Jude, did you remember your Indian costume?" Stephanie asked.

"Got it right here." I patted my bag.

The dress rehearsal took all afternoon, beginning with first grade right after lunch. Finally the sixth-graders stood at the edge of the stage, jostling about, dressed in our complete Pilgrim and Indian costumes. Randy looked straight at me as he pulled off his hat and adjusted his wide stiff collar. "I wish I could be an Indian instead of a stupid Pilgrim," he said.

"You do look kind of silly," I said. I pulled on my pigtail and waved it at him. "But it helps if you have these if you want to look like a real Indian."

"Quiet, everyone," said Mrs. Clark, clapping her hands. "Let's get started. We're about out of time." As we started running through our parts, I felt nervous about our actual performance coming up. What if I did something stupid or forgot my lines?

Saturday afternoon Dad sent me to the True Value Hardware to get some motor oil for the Wilsons' red Oldsmobile. He handed me an empty can so I'd know exactly what to get. He lay back down on the little sliding sled he used to work underneath cars. "Hurry back," he said. "I've got to have this Oldsmobile done by four o'clock for big lawyer Wilson."

Dad had fixed my tire, so I rode my bike downtown. When I walked into True Value, the old building came alive with sound. Bells jingled when I opened the door and crystal figurines tinkled as I walked over the ancient floorboards. I was curious about the new items that filled one side of the display window—bridal wear, tuxes, formal dresses. I shrugged my shoulders. Mr. Lipton must be branching out.

I circled through the store until I found the oil. There was no one nearby to help me so I started reading the labels. None looked exactly like the one Dad gave me, so I tried to match up the kinds. 10W30, 10W40. I heard two men's voices in the next aisle. I recognized the voice of Mr. Miller, the janitor from the school, talking to another man from town.

Mr. Miller said, "I heard these kids even painted words on the side of the school, here and over at Tri-County."

The other man said, "Probably the same kids that stole the signs."

"Most likely. That kid they arrested lives with Wilson the lawyer. Also got him for marijuana. They say there's still about five signs missing in the area. You could probably go to jail for doing that."

I'd heard enough. I picked up four cans of 10W30 and hurried to the counter.

CHAPTER 17

October 1938
Tuesday

AFTER THEIR UNEASY TRUCE, RUSSELL AND DANNY WERE BACK IN THE fields on Tuesday. They delivered a load of corn to the elevator, picked up the Monday newspaper, and returned home to find Devore out in the field with the plane. The sun was shining but the air was cool, a few clouds like brushstrokes high in the sky.

"I found you some jet fuel in Lafayette," Devore said. "You're all filled up, ready to go." He patted the side of the plane.

"Weather willing, I'll take off tomorrow. If it's like today it'll be perfect." Danny rubbed his hands together.

Devore counted the money that Danny placed in his hand, thanked him, and walked back through the field to his truck. Danny and Russ stayed by the plane.

"I think I'll drive her over to the road and take off from there," Danny said, pointing across the field to the straight gray line that marked the dirt road. "Use it as a runway, so to speak."

"Sounds good," Russ said. "Think you ought to leave today? It's nice and dry."

"Well, if you don't mind, I'd like to spend one last night with you. I told the girls I'd treat them to a movie in town. They have an early evening show for children on Tuesdays."

"Let me talk to Mary," Russ said, turning away. "But tomorrow you go. I think it will be better for everybody." He walked alone across the field to the house.

"Russ, he answered all our questions yesterday," Mary said, taking Russ's hand in hers.

"He always has an answer for everything, I'll guarantee that."

"I think he's good at heart, Russ. He's already told the girls about the movie and they're so excited about it. They think the world of him."

"It goes against my better judgment, Mary," he said, his mouth firm. He looked down at Mary and his voice softened. "But he's leaving tomorrow and he does know how I feel about things." He pushed his shoulders back. "I told him pretty straight."

Mary squeezed Russ's hand. "Thank you," she said.

Russell sat at the table with his account book after supper while Ellen and Rita rushed through their chores and school lessons. Now they stood waiting in the kitchen in their Sunday dresses, coats folded over their arms.

"Look how excited they are," Mary said to Russ.

Danny entered the room, dressed in his leather jacket, gray pants, white shoes. He spread the *Rensselaer Republican* on the kitchen table.

"Did you see the paper, girls?" Ellen and Rita leaned forward to read the big headlines about the aviator that landed in the Walstra cornfield. It was on the front page, picture and all.

"We're going to the show with someone famous," Ellen said, eyes bright.

Russell and Mary watched Danny escort the girls to the car, making a great show of bowing and opening the door for them like a chauffeur. The girls giggled and waved good-bye.

Mary waved back at them from the door.

Russ said, "I've harnessed the wagon in back of the barn. We're following them." He grabbed his jacket off the hook by the door.

Mary looked over at him. "Russ? Really, can't you—"

"I still don't trust him."

In minutes they were in the wagon and trailing after the car. When they reached town, they passed by their car, which was parked in front of C.W. Peck's store, and stopped the wagon down the street, just around the corner. They watched Danny and the girls come out of the store, each girl holding one of Danny's hands. Ellen carried a small paper sack. They walked to the theater, Danny stood at the window to buy the tickets, and then they went inside.

"Now what," Mary said. "Are we going to sit here for two hours?"

"No, reckon not," Russell said. "Let's go home." He didn't really have a plan.

They were sitting up waiting when the moviegoers returned at nine thirty.

"We saw *Lost Horizon*," Ellen said. "It was about a plane that crashes in the mountains and they discover a lost land that no one has seen before."

"Let's don't dwell on plane crashes." Danny laughed. "But that bit about discovering a lost land, that sounds like me landing here in Remington."

Mary laughed. "Oh, come now." Her eyes twinkled.

Russell shifted from one foot to another but said nothing.

"We had fun," Rita said. "Danny got us some candy." She held up the sack.

"Off to bed," Russ said. "School tomorrow."

Danny gave Ellen and Rita a hug. "I'll be flying back to Chicago tomorrow if the weather's fit."

Russell nodded. "Yep, should be a good day for it."

The girls turned their heads together toward their father. He knew what they wanted. He looked at Mary, who was also waiting for an answer. "And yes, you can stay home from school to watch." He felt like he'd been defeated at a county debate, twice in one day.

CHAPTER 18

Fall 1968

I WORRIED ABOUT WHAT I'D HEARD IN THE HARDWARE STORE. WAS BRAD A criminal, would Marty get in trouble? I wanted to ask Marty about it, but he wasn't around. I called Kristy, but no one answered.

Lana called later. "Did you hear about Brad Wilson?"

"Yes, I'm worried about Kristy. And Marty."

"Why Marty?"

"He's Brad's friend."

"Well, it just proves my point."

"What point?"

"About Kristy."

I didn't want to argue with her. It was no use.

That evening I sat quietly in the car next to Dad as we drove the few blocks to the basketball game, Marty's first home game.

"I heard Wilson's son, or brother, or whatever he is, got arrested," he said. He looked over at me.

"I don't know much about him," I said. I realized now that the news must be all over town.

As we entered the three-story brick building, Dad said, "This is the last year for this old school. The new high school at Tri-County is supposed to be finished by next fall."

I looked at the date etched in the cornerstone. "It was built in 1907," I said. "Sixty-one years ago."

Dad continued, "Your mom went to school here, and so did your grandma and grandpa Walstra. It would have been brand-new for them."

We entered the gym and sat together on the bleachers. The gym floor gleamed with polish. Only about a third of the seats were filled for the junior varsity games, but a much bigger crowd would be there for the varsity game.

The Remington Rifles usually lost to Rensselaer, and tonight was no different. Rensselaer won the JV game 54 to 38. I didn't actually watch the game because I left Dad soon after we sat down and sat with Trudy. Her brother Dan was a junior, so she was always there. She didn't mention anything about Brad, so maybe not everyone in town knew. We moved from place to place, walked down to the concession stand, talked to kids in the hallways. I kept looking for Randy and Kristy, but neither of them came. I wondered what would happen to Brad. And Marty, too. Adventure was one thing, but jail was another.

I looked up at the crowd between games and saw that Mr. and Mrs. Kaminsky were sitting next to Dad. At least Dad wasn't sitting alone and the Kaminskys probably didn't want to sit alone either. They had changed, I thought, since Steven was gone. Trudy said they didn't even make a fuss about her steady boyfriend. She was changing, too, now that she was in ninth grade. Our age difference seemed greater. We sat down with some of her new friends during the varsity game. Two high school girls, Bobbi and Jill, came over at half-time and stood by me.

Bobbi asked, "Are you Marty's sister? I think he's so cute." She pulled her hair back behind her ear, her eyes not on me but roaming the gym.

"Yeah, I'm his sister."

I tried to see my brother the way they did. Maybe they liked his careless attitude, the way he ignored them, or the way his hair flopped down over his eyes when it wasn't cut short for basketball season. And he was one of the best players on the team.

"What's he doing after the game?"

"I don't know. Probably going home."

The only reason they talked to me was because of Marty. For the first time I wondered if that was why Kristy talked to me. Was I so stupid I hadn't seen it?

After the varsity game, which we lost 61 to 49, I joined Dad to wait for Marty. We walked out on the floor to meet him as he came out of the locker room, rubbing his hand over his bristle of hair, carrying his tan gym bag.

"Great game," said Dad. "You looked good."

Marty looked up. "We lost. I could have done better. I shouldn't have tried that one shot."

Dad said, "You're right, but you scored eleven points." He skimmed his hand over the top of Marty's head. "Keep working and learn to play smart. Next year you'll be on varsity. Keep it up and maybe you can get a scholarship."

"Why don't they just move you up to varsity now?" I asked.

Dad said, "The coach knows what he's doing."

I saw the group of high school girls, including Bobbi and Jill, watching the boys come out. Some of them went out to meet their boyfriends.

I didn't tell Marty the girls had asked about him, and I don't think he really cared. Basketball was more important to him right now.

Back home, Marty opened the refrigerator door as soon as we entered the kitchen. He stood before it awhile and then grabbed a gallon of milk and a package of bologna. I washed a plastic bowl and poured out some cereal, while Dad and Marty made sandwiches and opened a can of peanuts. Hooking his gym bag onto his arm, Marty carried his sandwich and a large glass of milk upstairs. I took my bowl and followed him all the way into his room.

"Hey, I heard some guys in the hardware store today. They said Brad was arrested for stealing signs." I hesitated, and then said slowly, "and for marijuana."

"I know it." He set his food down and threw his gym bag to the floor.

"Will he go to jail?"

"Probably just have to pay a fine. I don't know, Jude. I'm not the police."

"Well, we can't afford to pay a fine if you get in trouble."

Sunday evening we gathered at the Methodist church for our annual Thanksgiving basket giveaway. The baskets, with ingredients for a complete turkey dinner, would be delivered to people who were considered needy. I went with Aunt Rita and Lana because they said it would be good for me. Mom had always helped with things like this and they didn't want me to miss out. We went down to the basement, where boxes of food sat on tables in a row like an assembly line. I heard a commotion behind us on the stairs. Someone was coming down carrying a leaning tower of wicker baskets.

"Watch out, here I come," a man's voice cried out from behind the tower.

I recognized Pastor Landauer as the baskets spilled out onto the floor. He just laughed. "No harm done. Welcome, everyone. Thank you for coming." He always brought joy into a room.

A small table stood along the wall bearing a coffee urn, plates of desserts, and a sweating canister of iced tea. I grabbed a cookie as Pastor Landauer walked up to the table after picking up all his baskets.

"Help yourself," Mary Reed said.

Her sister Martha chimed in, "I made my pumpkin bars, Pastor."

"Just like Mary and Martha in the Bible," he said, picking up a stack of cookies.

Mary in her flowered apron blushed as she reached up to touch her white hair bun. Martha bustled about in sturdy black shoes.

After the baskets were filled, the men carried them upstairs and placed them in the waiting cars. Aunt Rita had four baskets to deliver, one to the Antorettis with the big family, one to the Mayhughs, one to Susan Burke who was raising two babies by herself, and lastly, one to Old Herb.

"He's just a lonely old man," Aunt Rita said as we parked in front of his house.

"What's Old Herb going to do with a whole turkey?" Lana asked.

"We got him a small turkey roll. All he has to do is heat it up."

His house looked mysterious. "It's like he's trying to hide something in there." I said.

"Only thing he's hiding is himself," said Aunt Rita. "Who knows? He may want people to visit him."

"Maybe he just wants to be left alone," I said.

We walked together to the unpainted front door and Aunt Rita knocked.

"I don't think he's home," Lana said. She stepped up to the nearby window and put her face close to the glass.

"Oh, I think he's home," said Rita as she pulled Lana back. "Don't stare into people's windows, Lana."

Just then Old Herb pulled aside a gray lace curtain, startling us all. He opened the door.

"We brought you some Thanksgiving food from the Methodist church," Aunt Rita said, offering her most welcoming smile.

Lana and I held up the basket as best we could.

Old Herb had a blank look on his face. "I don't go to church."

"That's okay," Aunt Rita said. "Just consider it a blessing and you don't have to do anything in return. It's just the love of Jesus."

"Well, okay, set it down there." He motioned toward the floor of the porch.

Lana and I quickly lowered it down to the floor with a small thud.

Aunt Rita said, "God bless you," and we left. As we pulled away in the car, I looked back and watched Old Herb take a stiff step out onto his porch, pick up the basket, and set it inside.

"He took it," I reported.

"Sure, he did," Aunt Rita said. "Maybe it will soften up his heart again."

Back home in the kitchen, I asked Dad why Old Herb was so grouchy. Dad took dishes from the dish drainer and arranged them in the cupboards while I searched the refrigerator for something to eat. I found a Tupperware bowl containing Jell-O with fruit cocktail that Grandma had sent over.

"Well, you know Herb used to run the elevator with his brother Harold. He wasn't always a hermit like this. Things changed after Herb fell off the elevator roof and landed on a pile of machinery parts and junk. His leg was pretty smashed up and got sliced by a piece of sheet metal."

I squinted my eyes. "You mean it cut his leg off?"

"No, but it never healed right and they finally had to take it off. He was in a wheelchair, couldn't work, things got bad. He just got that artificial leg about two years ago. But it was too late. I guess he and Harold had some kind of dispute. They had financial problems at the elevator, and there was an argument and who knows what happened for sure. I think they made a deal and he got the house and his brother got the elevator. He seems to have gotten the bad end of the deal and doesn't talk to Harold anymore."

I put the Tupperware bowl in the sink.

He continued, "He does have family, but I don't think they have much to do with him. His wife divorced him, too."

"Maybe he's actually rich and has all his money hidden under his bed," I said.

"That's just your imagination running away with you, Jude. Too many mystery books. Real life is different." He shut the cupboard door. "I don't really know what to think about Old Herb now."

I remembered the one time Old Herb actually came to church. It was on "Invite a Friend Sunday." A lady named Bernice invited Old

Herb, and to everyone's surprise, he came. I watched that day as he entered the church dressed in a tweed suit coat over his work pants, with a denim shirt and one of those cowboy string ties. But he seemed so out of place there, and everyone stared at him. Then Bernice, who was so happy he'd actually come, rushed back to greet him and several ladies followed. Mom, too. Dad said we just smothered him and scared him away because he never came back. Dad said you've got to give people like that some room to breathe.

CHAPTER 19

October 1938
Wednesday

THE WALSTRAS AWOKE TO RAIN HAMMERING AGAINST THE WINDOWS. The plane would not be flying today. Mary watched Russ and Danny lean into the wind, hands on their hats, as they walked to the barn. It had turned colder overnight, with wind gusts that drove the remaining leaves to the ground.

The men came inside the house after milking, just as the girls were leaving to catch the hack waiting in the road.

"Won't be flying today, girls," Danny said.

"I know," Ellen said. "It means you can stay longer, but now we have to go to school." She frowned and dragged her feet, then hurried to catch up with her sister.

Mary placed a platter of fried mush on the table and sat next to Russ across from Danny.

"What took so long this morning?"

"Door on the barn was blown off. Had to fix the blame thing," Russ said. "Still haven't fed the stock." They ate in silence. Russell got up from the table, took his denim coat from the hook, put on his hat, and opened the door.

"The weather doesn't stop what I've got to do," he said as the wind slammed the door shut behind him.

"What does Russ do on rainy days like this?" Danny asked.

Mary picked up the plates and laughed lightly. "Always plenty to do. I imagine he'll be splitting wood for the kitchen stove after he feeds the stock."

Danny noted that the box by the stove was empty.

"At least the coal bin is full," she said. "Winter will be here soon enough."

"I've enjoyed my stay here, Mary." He watched her pour sugar into her tea, two spoons full.

"Oh, well, you just dropped in. What were we to do?" They laughed together.

She stirred her coffee without looking up. "It was a pleasure having you here. But I suppose you're anxious to get back to Chicago."

"Life goes on."

"What do you think will happen with you and Jean?"

"You win some, you lose some." He drank the rest of his coffee and set the cup down.

"People must think a little differently there in Chicago. You don't seem to care what happens next. Like you have no direction."

Danny laughed. "You may be right, but I always manage to come out on top." He stood up. "Guess I better go help Russ." He put on his coat and went out into the rain.

Mary sat for a moment listening to the rain as it ran off the roof of the house and streamed down the kitchen window. Heat radiated from the kitchen stove, and the wood hissed and popped. She roused herself and walked to the cupboard, dissolved some yeast in water, and measured out flour to begin her bread making for the week. She poured water into a pan and set it on the stove to heat up for washing dishes. She looked at the kerosene lamp, the pile of dirty clothes on the back porch, and through the window to the rain turning the yard into mud. What was it like to live in a city like Chicago? What would it be like not to be so completely at the mercy of the weather, to have electricity. Familiar tears rose up in her eyes. She'd felt this way before, though, and knew she'd get over it. She lifted her apron and wiped her cheek. She thought of her girls and Russ. She thought of the little gravestone past the orchard. She thought of more children she might have someday, maybe sons.

The door opened suddenly, and Danny stepped inside followed by a gust of wind. He crossed the kitchen to the closed-in porch and returned, slapping a pair of gloves against his hand.

"Forgot my gloves," he said.

Mary turned around.

"Have you been crying? What's wrong?" he said.

"Oh, nothing. I get this way sometimes. It's nothing." She managed a smile.

"My goodness," he said. "Sit down."

She sat down on the chair as an obedient child. "Really, I'm fine. Just a little tired." She wiped her cheeks with her finger.

Danny took her hand. "You're a fine, beautiful woman. I'd help you if I could. I like the farm, but you have no help, no conveniences."

Mary gave in to tears. Danny put his arm around her shoulder. "I'd love to fly you away from here with me, but of course that's out of the question."

They both turned toward a noise behind them and watched as Russell shoved open the back door and stepped inside.

"The calves are loose…in the cornfield," he said, breathing heavily. His eyes widened and his face turned hard as he saw Danny and his wife huddled together. "What's going on here?"

Mary stood up and Danny stepped back against the cupboard.

"Nothing, sir."

"It's not what it looks like, Russell." Mary walked toward him.

Russell walked deliberately past her into the pantry and returned with the shotgun.

"Calves loose because of this fool, and now he's trying to…" Russell's voice was shaking. He pointed the gun toward Danny. "Don't you move."

Danny stood still as a statue.

Mary reached out her hand. "Russell, you're not thinking. Nothing was going on. I beg you."

Russell glared at Danny and waved the gun toward the door. "Now, get out there and get those calves."

"I'm sure I locked the gate."

"Well, you didn't. Shut up and get out there."

Danny pulled his coat off the hook and walked out the door, like a dog that'd been kicked.

Mary stood silently, afraid to say anything else. She had never seen Russell act this way. He cracked open the gun, pulled out the shell, and threw it skittering across the floor, where it rolled against the wall. He looked down at the gun, arms shaking. He walked to the pantry, shoved the gun inside, and slammed the door. He strode past Mary, avoiding her eyes, walked out the door, and crossed the yard to where Danny stood by the barn waiting in the rain.

The men returned about two hours later, soaked and streaked with mud. The calves were rounded up and back in the pen. Not a word was spoken again about the incident. Mary had composed herself and finished the bread. When it was baked and cooled, she cut thick slices for supper and placed it on the table next to the apple butter, hard-boiled eggs, and milk.

The girls returned from school and never knew that anything unusual had happened. After supper they gathered around the radio for a short time but went to bed early. Tomorrow would be another day.

CHAPTER 20

November 1968

SUNDAY NIGHT WHILE LYING IN BED, I THOUGHT OF THE COMING WEEK. Tuesday evening was our Thanksgiving play, Wednesday we only had a half day of school, then that evening the McCools would be coming and we'd go to Grandma's. Thursday was Thanksgiving Day, when we'd go to Aunt Rita's for turkey and dressing and cranberry salad and pumpkin pie. We wouldn't have to go back to school until the following Monday. It was a lot to be thankful for.

Monday I sat down by Kristy at the lunch table before the rest of her friends got there. She seemed quieter, not her usual self. She plowed right into her sandwich without saying anything.

"Are you worried about Brad?"

"Oh, him? My dad's a lawyer, he'll get him off." She said it so lightly, maybe she wasn't worried.

"What about Marty?"

She looked up from her lunch tray. "You mean, will Brad tell on him?"

I nodded my head.

"Don't worry. He won't squeal. He's been through this before."

"Before?"

"Oh, yeah." She rolled her eyes. "This is definitely not his first offense. That's why he came to live with us. Clean country air and all. Guess it didn't work. I don't really care what happens to him one way or the other." She opened her milk carton and stuck in a straw.

Rhonda and Carol sat down with us so we changed the subject.

That night I talked to Marty again. He was washing the kitchen trash can because something had leaked and it smelled like a dead animal. Dad made him do it.

"I talked to Kristy today. She says Brad won't tell on you."

"He better not, that punk."

"Shouldn't you do something about those signs? It's evidence."

"I will. I'll return them as soon as I can get Dad's truck and no one's around."

He paused, thinking. "So, maybe when we're at Grandma's on Wednesday when those people are here, I'll have Eddie call me saying I need to return his wallet or something. Like he left it in my gym bag in his jacket. Then I'll go back, get the signs, take the stop sign out by the railroad, and then just run the rest out to the highway department by the interstate. No one will be there in the evening."

"Can I go with you?"

"No. Have you told anyone?"

"No"

Tuesday morning I was nervous about our play as I checked myself in the bathroom mirror. We had practiced many times during school and I knew my lines, but I had never been in a play like this before. I was also a little concerned about Kristy, the way she seemed a little cold on Monday. I was probably another of her throwaways who didn't measure up. At least I had my chance and gave it my best try. Too bad I'd pulled away from Lana and Lydia. I hardly talked to them anymore. There was still Stephanie and always Trudy.

I stood before the full-length mirror that was propped against the wall. I was completely dressed. I was Running Bear in tan tights, vest, loincloth, braided hair, feathers, beads. I held my hands in front of me as if holding a basket of corn and practiced my lines.

My name is Running Bear. I have brought corn to share in this meal of thanksgiving... We can live together in peace. We have much to share with each other... And my last line, *Let us be thankful for this year's harvest.*

Next would be the poem I would recite with the other Indians, and that would be easy to remember. I tried speaking with different tones of voice, at different speeds, and only felt more nervous. I looked at my outfit, though, and had to admit it looked authentic to me.

Dad called, "Ready, Blue Jay?"

"Guess so," I called out.

I put on shoes and long pants, winter coat over the top, and walked out to the car where Dad and Marty waited. It was already getting dark, the sky dull gray, heavy with clouds that suggested snow.

We entered the elementary school, and I walked down the hallway toward the cafeteria while Dad and Marty turned right to go to the gym.

I slowed down and looked at the kindergarten and first grade artwork lining the hall, hand-shaped turkeys with tails colored like the rainbow. I ran my hand along the yellow brick walls.

I clearly remembered walking down these halls at each grade level with Mom.

I remembered my first day of kindergarten. I had all new clothes, so eager to get started. Mom had cried. She said her little girl was growing up too fast.

At age five I told her, "You've got to let me grow up, Mom."

"I know," she said, and gave me such a big, long hug I had to pull away before she made a scene.

And here I was in sixth grade without her. Pressure built up in my head as I stopped the tears. I speeded up, shaking the thoughts from my head. I walked quickly past second-grade Pilgrims cut from black and white construction paper, pale watercolor Indians at third grade. The hallway became more crowded with my classmates as we reached the cafeteria. I was back to normal.

Mrs. Norman stood at the door and directed me to the area where the sixth-graders were assembled. When everyone was accounted for, we filed into the gym, starting with the first-graders, and took our seats in the folding chairs placed in rows over a brown tarpaulin. Lana and Stephanie were right behind me dressed as Indians, Lydia was further back, while Randy and Kristy, both Pilgrims, were toward the front of the line.

"I feel stupid in this loincloth," Lana said. "We look naked with these tan tights." She adjusted her loincloth to cover as much skin as possible.

When everyone was seated, the lights were dimmed and Mr. Peake, the principal, entered the stage. I craned my head around until I found Dad and Marty sitting toward the middle, right in the center. Dad smiled at me and raised his hand in a little wave.

Mr. Peake urged the student body to quiet down and then thanked all the parents for their support and talked for several more minutes. Mrs. Norman started in on the piano, which was the cue for the first-graders to stand and file out to the left, up the stairs, and onto the lighted stage. They lined up in two rows, tall kids to the back, and sang a song about the food of Thanksgiving. They returned to their seats, and each grade performed in turn until it was time for the sixth-grade play.

We shuffled out and stood in the hallway to wait while the fifth grade performed. Standing there, I realized how badly I needed to go the bathroom, so I asked Mr. Peake and he said to hurry. I ran to the girls' bathroom and returned to where the class now stood in the darkened wings of the stage. The curtains swished closed while the fifth-grade boys changed the scenery.

It was time for us. The curtains opened to reveal two teepees and a long wooden table. The forest backdrop that I'd help to paint looked beautiful, I thought. The Pilgrims entered first. Kristy and the other Pilgrim women carried baskets of food to the table and placed pots over the fake fire, which was Rita's invention made of tissue paper over a light bulb. Randy and the Pilgrim men walked to the front of the stage holding their muskets. They spoke to the audience about the successful harvest and how they survived their first winter. They were especially thankful that the Indians showed them how to grow corn and fertilize it with fish. That was the signal for the four main Indian braves to enter, which included me. As we walked into the light, I heard a slight titter in the audience. I felt my loincloth being yanked and felt cloth rushing past my bare skin. I whirled around as Lana pulled out the rear flap of my loincloth, which I had apparently stuffed into my flesh-colored tights when I was in the bathroom. It must have looked like a round bare bottom glowing in those lights. I was horrified. I looked out to the audience to see if they had seen anything, but the floor lights were so bright I saw only blackness beyond. I knew there were people there, people I knew and my own family. I remembered hearing that tittering sound and knew they had seen.

I forgot what to do next. Lana rescued me by whispering my lines and I spoke out. "My name is Running Bear…"

Lana told me later that I did say my lines, but all I remember was a loud humming in my ears and my face a blaze of heat.

After my part was over, I remember Randy and the Pilgrims praying that there would always be peace and understanding between their people and ours. I know we said the poem, we sang the Tom Turkey song, and then we filed off the stage. The play was over.

I found Dad and Uncle Phil out in the hall. Aunt Rita held on to the twins who were dressed alike in brown pants and knitted vests over white shirts. I asked Dad how stupid I looked.

He said, "Oh, that. I'm sure no one noticed."

"You and Lana were great," Uncle Phil said. "Little goof-ups only make a play more fun."

Aunt Rita joined in. "There were lots of funny things that happened. Most of those first-graders didn't sing at all, just looked around. So cute. And there was a second-grade boy that sneezed on the girl in front of him and she turned around and hit him."

"But those are little kids. I'm in sixth grade."

"You were the best Indian out there," Dad said.

"Parents always say nice things to make their kids feel better."

"Blue Jay, you made a boring play more exciting," Dad said with a smile and a wink.   He put his arm around me. "Oh, by the way. The McCools are already here. They came a day early and were here at the program." His eyes scanned the crowd. "They must have gone already with Grandma."

That was the last straw. Danny McCool saw me. He must think I'm an idiot. When we got home, I went straight to bed.

School let out at noon on Wednesday, and not soon enough for me. I walked home alone. It was one of those dreary days that could get you down, but we were off for Thanksgiving and no one said anything embarrassing that day about my loincloth problem. Randy thought it was funny, but I actually enjoyed the teasing from him.

On my way home I saw a little blue car in front of Old Herb's house parked behind Herb's rusty red truck. It looked like the Mayhughs' car. As I passed by, I looked through the fence and tangle of bushes like I always did and saw little Bobby in a corduroy overcoat petting the cats that collected around Old Herb's house.

It got me thinking. So maybe Caroline was his family that never came around; maybe she was his daughter.

I stared.

Caroline pleaded with her father, "The church is an okay place to stay, but I know you've got money hidden here. I'll never get any money from that good-for-nothing father of the girls. I know you've got money stashed somewhere."

"What you doing?"

It was Lydia. I hadn't seen her behind the shaggy cedar tree.

"What are you doing here?" I threw it right back to her.

"Do you care?" She seemed hurt. Lana had probably turned her against me.

"You don't have to be mean," I said.

Lydia picked up Bobby and went inside Old Herb's house. I went home.

I walked into the kitchen about suppertime. Normally on the day before Thanksgiving, Mom would be putting pumpkin pies in the oven and would have ginger cookies cooling in straight rows on sheets of wax paper. There were no welcoming aromas in the kitchen today. I opened the refrigerator, but there was not much more than a bowl of hard-boiled eggs, a pitcher of Kool-Aid, and a few plastic containers with unknown contents.

Dad walked in the door. "Never fear, Jude. I just got groceries."

He set two sacks on the counter and handed me a box of Hamburger Helper. "Want to fix that for supper?"

I read the instructions on the back and put some water in a pan to boil, then opened a package of hamburger.

"After we eat, we have to go over to Grandma's to see the McCools."

"I'm so embarrassed about the play, but I really do want to meet him."

Dad put a new bottle of dish soap by the sink. "What for?"

"I want to ask him what it was like to fly a plane in World War II and what the war was like. And about NASA and going to the moon."

"Well, hold your horses. He probably doesn't have anything to do with going to the moon. But I guess when it comes to him, you never know. I guess we'll find out what ole Danny McCool's up to these days." He winked at me. "I'm going for the cookies."

"Me, too." I stirred the hamburger as it browned in the skillet.

Dad took plates and silverware out of the dish drainer and placed them on the table. He opened up a jar of dill pickles and sat down.

"I remember when that plane was sitting there in Grandpa's field. Your mom brought water and apples out to the field for me and Mr. Devore. Your mom was a little younger than me. She wore dresses most of the time, back then. I lived in Rensselaer and worked at Devore's garage, my first job. I thought I was mature, but heck, I was only sixteen. Same age as Marty. Can you imagine Marty seeming mature?"

"No." I laughed and took a pickle out of the jar. "He doesn't even have a real job." I loved it when Dad sat and talked to me like this.

"I was excited to get to work on an airplane. All I'd ever done was pump gas and change oil in cars. I got to meet a real pilot, but I don't know how good of a pilot he was. Folks in town thought he was taking advantage of people. Ended up I spent more time talking to your mom. And I didn't really work that much on the airplane, just handed tools to Mr. Devore and watched. I thought your mom was cute the way she was so shy but wanted to hang around and see what was going on."

"Serendipity," I said. "It was serendipity. You were looking for one thing and found another."

"I guess so, Blue Jay."

CHAPTER 21

October 1938
Friday

THE GROUND WAS DRY AFTER THE RAIN ON WEDNESDAY, THE WIND calm, the sky deep blue. Good flight weather. Danny stood in the kitchen, zipped up his leather flight jacket, slipped on the aviator hat, snapped his goggles around his forehead. He was ready. He was satisfied the airplane was in good working order after revving the engine in the misty dawn and driving the plane in a circle around the mown alfalfa field next to the cornfield. He had checked and rechecked everything he could think of. The girls, home from school for the occasion, were waiting by the door.

"We're just waiting for Brady," Russ said. "He's got to have his pictures for the paper, you know."

Danny went into the closed-in porch where he'd spent the week to gather his bags. Mary followed.

She had been silent all morning, but now she spoke to him.

"I hope you won't think badly of Russ. The calves could have damaged the corn or eaten too much and died. We can't afford any more loss. I don't blame you, either. I've always felt you have a good heart. I would like you to take this, though."

She handed him a paper folded in half. "Just because a woman cries doesn't mean she's without hope. I know my place in the world, and I hope you find yours. I told you I thought you needed some

169

direction…for life…so I wrote down some things that might help you. Things that have helped me."

"Thank you, Mary." He took the paper, folded it into a small square, and put it in his shaving kit.

"You'll read it?"

"I'll do it for you."

Brady came and they walked to the field. Just like the day he landed, Danny McCool posed in front of the plane, arm resting on a wing, and again gave his interview to Brady. He enjoyed the feeling of being in the news. Devore was there, too, giving his report, smiling for his picture.

Finally, Danny stepped into the plane and everyone formed a small group off to the side. Mary stood with the girls on either side of her, Russ behind with his arms across his chest. Danny started the engine and waved out the window like a celebrity as the plane eased across the field and onto the gravel road. He turned up the engines, rolled along the road picking up speed, and then lifted into the air.

From the ground, the Walstras watched the plane make a wide loop above their heads, dip a wing as if saying good-bye, and then head north. It soon became a tiny dot against the blue sky and then disappeared.

CHAPTER 22

November 1968

WEDNESDAY EVENING WE DRESSED TO MEET THE McCOOLS. Marty was wearing a black T-shirt with PURDUE stamped across the front in gold letters.

"Mr. McCool will love this shirt." He slapped his chest.

Dad hurried down the stairs behind him.

"You might want to dress up a little more for company, Marty." Dad looked at me and his face softened. "Jude, you look very pretty."

I felt good in my brown bell bottoms and fuzzy cream-colored sweater, my favorite outfit. Marty turned around and ran back upstairs.

"It's snowing outside, so you'll need coats," Dad said. He opened the door and stepped onto the porch.

I looked through the living room window, and sure enough I saw flakes in the circle of light surrounding the lamppost. It wasn't sticking to the ground, though. I saw Dad cross the yard to start the car. Marty came downstairs pulling a green sweater over his T-shirt.

"Can I help you return those signs?" I said.

"No, but just back me up if anybody asks questions. I'll be getting a phone call and I'll say I'm leaving to take Eddie his coat and billfold. I'll take the stop sign out to the railroad crossing where we got it and return the others to the highway department and be right back."

"Okay, I'll help you out." It was the first time he'd ever trusted me to do something for him. It was like I was part of the plan.

We drove the two miles to Grandma Walstra's farm. Aunt Rita and Uncle Phil's Ford was already there, and a black Buick, the McCools' car, was parked behind it. The twins were outside, reaching out to the sky trying to catch snowflakes that melted as soon as they hit their warm hands.

When we entered the living room, the McCools stood up to greet us. Grandma introduced us all to each other and we shook hands. I have to say I was surprised at how old Mr. McCool looked. He leaned on a cane, a fancy one with carvings like a totem pole, and was wearing a gray sweater that buttoned up the front, the kind an old man would wear. His gray hair made him look tired. His wife was younger, but it was hard to tell for sure with her makeup and dyed hair.

Mr. McCool was charming, though, even if he was old.

"So, this is Marty, the basketball player," he said. "I've already heard all about you." This made Marty stand up tall until Mr. McCool patted him on the back so hard he wavered forward.

"Used to play a little myself, but that was long ago." His laugh was what you would expect from Santa Claus.

Marty said, "Thanks, yeah, I hope to make varsity next year."

"And you must be Judy, the actor. I saw you in the play last night." He looked straight at me, the skin around his eyes wrinkling in a hundred places, his eyes the palest gray. "Fine job," he said.

"Thanks," was all I could manage. I walked directly to one of the dining room chairs placed in the living room for the kids and sat down. He spoke something clever to everyone else, even Uncle Phil.

Finally everyone sat down and Dad turned to Grandma. "Well, what do we have to drink?"

"I've got coffee, regular and decaf, 7-Up, and Dr Pepper," Grandma said.

Aunt Rita motioned for me and Lana to help.

I was glad to get up and have something to do. I felt like a waitress, taking everyone's orders and then balancing the cups and glasses on Grandma's silver tray. I held the tray like a statue while Lana handed out each drink.

"My, what lovely hostesses," Mrs. McCool said. Danny followed with, "I remember, Judy, how your mother kept us supplied with apples when we were working on that plane back in '38. Kept bringing us bowls of apples." He stopped smiling and turned to Dad. "Let me say how sad I was to hear of the passing of Ellen."

Dad shifted in his chair but said, "Thank you."

It made me feel sad but it also felt good to hear someone talk about Mom.

It was quiet for a while, and then Grandma said, "No one ever landed a plane in our cornfield before…or since." Everyone laughed.

Rita said, "I remember vaguely, but I was only seven. I wasn't allowed to go out there all the time like Ellen was."

"It was quite an event for us country folk," Grandma added.

"Let me get the cookies," Rita said. She walked out to the kitchen and returned with the tray of ginger cookies and snickerdoodles. She set them on the coffee table next to a stack of orange napkins.

"That was quite a time. It was the beginning of this friendship, too," said Danny McCool.

"We've written back and forth all these years," Grandma said, "and now you're here, and Doris, too. I thought that maybe God had a purpose in you landing here that day." She looked straight at Danny McCool.

Dad said, "Well, I met Ellen there." He reached for the tray and picked up six cookies, three of each kind. "Though, maybe I'd have met her at the county fair or somewhere later anyway."

Rita said, "No, you met her there and I think that was God's plan."

Dad held up a hand. "I won't argue with that." He put a cookie in his mouth.

The phone rang. Marty's head jerked as Grandma picked up the phone. "Yes." She held the phone out in the air. "It's for you, Marty."

Marty crossed the room and took the phone from her. "Okay, I can do that. Okay, soon as I can. 'Bye." He faced the room. "My friend Eddie says he left his coat in my gym bag and his billfold is in there. So I'm sorry, but I need to return it to him. Now."

"Why would his coat be in your gym bag?" Dad asked. He looked puzzled. "Can't it wait until tomorrow? We just got here."

"He said they're leaving tonight," Marty said. "They're going to see some relatives. For Thanksgiving, of course. Tomorrow. And his money is in there."

I tried to help out. "Eddie's dad gets mad if Eddie loses things, especially money."

Marty continued, "I'll just take the truck and be right back."

"Well, be careful, it's snowing," Dad said.

"I know." Marty grabbed his coat and left through the back door.

Uncle Phil turned to Mr. McCool. "So, I hear you were in the big war. I presume you flew fighter planes."

"Well, as you know, I was already a pilot when I joined the Air Force. After I got more training, they sent me overseas." Danny Mc-Cool picked up two cookies and laid them on his napkin. "Strange thing, I never did fly in the war."

My mouth fell open.

"Funny story," he continued, "though it wasn't funny at the time. I went through all that training. Was sent to England in 1944. We were just waiting, drilling, getting ready. Then one day, a crosswind caught one of our planes during a landing, a P 51 Mustang I believe, and it skidded into some barrels. And wouldn't you know, I was standing nearby and one of those barrels shot straight at me, knocked me over a concrete fence, broke my leg, and injured my back. I was in the hospital for months and then sent home. I can talk about it now, but for years I couldn't look a wounded veteran in the eye. You know, the ones with real injuries, from combat. My injury was from doing nothing but being at the wrong place at the wrong time."

The room was silent and then Grandma said, "Well, you were still there and would have given your life for your country. You were serving your country when it happened."

Mrs. McCool added, "That's right, that's what I tell him. And he's come to terms with it now." She patted his knee. "And he gets around fairly well with the cane."

"I'll drink to that," Mr. McCool said. He lifted his coffee cup and smiled. "To health!" We all lifted our glasses and cups into the air.

"Amen," said Grandma.

"Yes, amen," he said. "You know, one thing that helped me during the war and that long recovery?" We all looked to him, waiting.

He opened up his billfold, pulled out a little square of paper, and unfolded it on his knee. It looked like it had been folded many times. "This was given to me thirty years ago."

"Is it a clue?" I jumped up and walked toward him. Everyone laughed.

Dad said, "I keep telling you, everything's not a mystery, Judy."

"No, it's not a mystery," Mr. McCool said. "When I was a young man who thought he knew everything, when I really knew nothing at all, your grandma gave this to me, Judy." He looked to Grandma Walstra, who put her hand to her mouth.

"You kept that?" she said.

"Yes, it kept me going through the war." We all turned from Grandma to Mr. McCool.

"Well, what's it say?" said Phil.

Mr. McCool smoothed out the slip of paper and read.

If you want to have direction in your life, find a Bible and read Proverbs. Do what it says and it will keep you out of trouble. Read the Psalms to know how to pray, and read the Gospels to know the truth. Mary Walstra

These were things I knew from Sunday school. This was what got him through the war?

Grandma said, "Well, I never knew whether it made a difference or not. My goodness." She seemed a little overwhelmed by it all.

"It did make a difference," Mr. McCool said. "Someone, I forget who, gave me a little New Testament before I left the country. It included the Psalms and Proverbs. Kept it in my rucksack. Didn't really take your message and the New Testament seriously until I was flat on my back in the hospital. Had plenty of time to think then. I took it to heart."

"But you did fly in those fighter planes, those Mustangs. Before the injury?" I asked.

"Oh yes, it was grand. I would have gone over on D-day. We practiced flying those little planes. They sure seem small compared to today's planes. But they could do anything you wanted. Turn on a dime. Nothing like it, just you and your plane. I wish I could have fought."

Rita offered, "Maybe it was meant to be that you didn't go. Most of those pilots didn't make it."

Phil said, "You never know. I mean, who really knows?" He threw his hands into the air.

Everyone was quiet again, and then Grandma stood up. "It just shows God works in mysterious ways. My cup runneth over. More coffee, anyone?" Several held up their coffee cups, and Grandma went into the kitchen.

I looked at Danny McCool. "What about England? What was that like?"

"My, my, what an inquisitive little girl... I hope you plan to go to college with a mind like that."

I looked over to Dad. He had talked about Marty going to college if he could get a sports scholarship, but I had never considered it for me. Dad shrugged his shoulders. I turned back to Mr. McCool.

"To answer your question, Judy, we had a little time to sightsee and I liked England. All that history, the kings and queens. But the food, totally tasteless. Lots of mushy cabbage and potatoes boiled to death in plain water with no seasonings, sugarless puddings. I'm telling you I was glad to get back to the USA and good cooking." He patted Doris on the arm.

"Were they bombing England when you were there?" Phil asked.

"Oh my, there were still air raids. Scared us to death, though they weren't near as bad as in the Blitz in '41. You could see places in London that were just level to the ground from the Blitz. We'd use the underground tube to travel in London because it was so cheap, and it was amazing to see all the people in the evening, people whose homes were destroyed and the ones who were still afraid of air raids, sleeping in those underground tunnels. They would bring their own bedding and live in there at night. There weren't enough beds, and people would just sleep on the cement. But in the morning, those British people would come out with a smile and didn't seem to mind. They would even joke about it." He shook his head. "You've got to hand it to those British chaps for bravery."

We listened as Danny McCool told story after story. We forgot Marty still hadn't returned.

Mr. McCool drained his coffee cup and held it out to Grandma. "Boy, you're making me thirsty. Could I have some plain water? Just put it in here."

Grandma took his cup.

"Don't you work for NASA now?" I asked. "What do you do there?"

Before he could answer, a loud, crackling noise came from Dad's CB radio.

"Got it," Dad said and held out his hand as if to hold people away. He walked into the kitchen.

Mr. McCool leaned toward me. "Judy, I do work for NASA…"

"He's a bean counter," Mrs. McCool whispered loudly with her hand up to the side of her mouth like she was telling us a secret.

"What's a bean counter?" I was totally confused.

Dad returned from the kitchen, coat in hand, deep lines all over his forehead.

"There's an accident just outside of town. Involves the train."

Lana turned to me, her face white. "Those pennies!"

I looked at her. "No, it's Marty. The signs."

"What signs?"

"Never mind."

My mind quickly tried to cover all the bases. What if someone hit a train because the stop sign wasn't there, or what if Marty was hit somehow while he was putting the sign back?

Dad crossed the room and opened the front door. Police and fire truck sirens wailed in the night.

I stepped up beside him. "I'm going with you, Dad."

"No, you stay here."

Danny McCool rose from his seat, leaning against his cane.

"Wait," Dad said, standing in front of the door. "I don't have my truck. Marty has it."

"Dad, I need to talk to you."

"Not now, Jude." His voice was firm.

Grandma said, "You can take my car. It's in the garage. The keys are in it."

Dad stepped outside, pushing the door behind him, but it snapped back on a gust of wind. Cold air and snowflakes rushed inside. Grandma moved quickly to shut the door and then stood up straight in front of it.

I was reminded of that other night. The night Mom died there was a thin crescent moon in the western sky, sharp and cold with jagged edges like a torn fingernail. I know because I was on the front porch staring at it, waiting for her to come home. It was March 9, 1967, the day before my tenth birthday. Mom went to Rensselaer to shop for my birthday presents that afternoon, and it was getting late. It was time for supper, it was getting dark, Dad and Marty were looking for something to eat.

The police car drove up. Chief Martin got out. I ran into the house. Dad told me to go upstairs. I knew something was wrong.

Dad told me later what Chief Martin said. Mom died instantly. A deer ran across the road in front of her on 231. There was no way to avoid it. The hoof went through the windshield. She'd lost control and rolled down the embankment. The car, the green Gremlin, was totaled. They found my birthday presents in the backseat, gift-wrapped and all ready.

Grandma continued to stand in front of the door. "I hope no one was hurt. I pray Marty's all right."

Phil walked over to her. "I'm sure he's fine. The odds of getting hit by a train are like getting hit by lightning. Very small, probably half of one percent."

Rita frowned. "Phil, not now."

"I'm just saying." He held up his hands and then dropped them to his side.

Danny McCool walked around Grandma and opened the door, coat and hat on. "I'm going with him," he said. Grandma and Rita held hands to pray.

I grabbed my coat and slipped out behind him before anyone could stop me. The snow was falling faster now, big flakes that stuck to the grass.

"I need to come, too," I yelled toward Dad, who was struggling with the garage door. "I need to tell you something."

"I don't think it's a good idea, Jude." The door slid upward in jerks.

I ran past Danny McCool. "I'll just sit in the car," I said, pulling my hood up over my head. "It's one of those times I need to get back up on the horse." I knew that comment would work if anything would.

"I'll sit with her in the car," Danny McCool said as he caught up with us. I looked up at my new ally.

Dad was in the driver's seat and turned the key in the ignition. He spoke in his irritated voice. "All right. I don't have time to argue, just get in."

I hopped in the backseat, and Mr. McCool climbed in beside me. He barely pulled his second foot in the door when Dad backed out of the garage and then spun forward. Mr. McCool's head bounced back as he managed to pull the door shut, but he was a good sport about it. "And we're off," he said. He placed one large hand onto the seat in front of him and smiled at me, deep crinkles at the corner of his eyes.

Dad was focused on the road ahead. We sped down the road.

"What did you want to say, Jude?" I could tell Dad wasn't happy that I was along, but he couldn't get mad with Mr. McCool there, too.

"I was just afraid that maybe Marty was involved in the accident."

"Why'd you think that?" He was definitely upset. "Anyway, that's him right there in front of us." Dad lifted his index finger toward the windshield.

Sure enough, the white truck was coming toward us, and Marty was waving at us to slow down. Dad began to roll down the window.

I heard Marty's voice whirl into the wind as we passed. "Accident back there…" Dad barely slowed down, just sent a dismissive wave out the window.

In the rearview mirror, I saw Marty making a three-point turn in the country road and start after us. All the fear left me as soon as I saw Marty was all right, but when I looked back at the truck again, I saw that Kristy sat beside him. Now I was just confused.

"Why do you kids think you have to be right in the middle of everything?" He slapped his hand against the steering wheel. I realized Dad was talking to me.

"You shouldn't be at the scene of an accident like this. Help me out, Mr. McCool. There's nothing exciting about a real accident."

I didn't know what to say, but then Mr. McCool put his arm around my shoulder.

"I'll watch out for Judy and cover her eyes if need be." He squeezed my shoulder.

I was beginning to love this old man. "Sorry, Dad. I just thought maybe it was Marty in the accident… No reason."

We turned right on the county road that was an extension of Railroad Street and headed down it, parallel to the train, which now sat stationary on the tracks. Dad's CB kept crackling with static and voices, but I couldn't understand anything. Lights flashed near the railroad crossing, and my heart raced knowing the gravity of all those red, blue, and white lights. We pulled off the road into tall grass and weeds behind the fire engine. Dad pushed the door open. He said, "Stay here," and ran off.

Danny McCool saluted quickly. "Yes, sir." But Dad didn't hear him. I watched Dad as he joined Chief Martin, who was talking into his CB. Men were running here and there. I was disoriented by the jumble of cars and people and by the odd brightness from the emergency lights. I didn't recognize the familiar railroad crossing.

Marty parked the white truck farther down the road. I could see him and Kristy sitting inside.

"Can we get out?" I asked.

"No, your dad's right. You shouldn't even be here, but I'll keep you company."

"I always wanted to meet you," I said. "I thought you were a war hero."

"It depends on what you mean by hero. Sometimes you're a hero just by surviving what life throws at you."

I considered what he said. It sounded like a true statement. "What's a bean counter?" I asked.

A laugh rumbled from Danny McCool, the friendly kind. "It means I was an accountant. I count numbers, like someone would count beans."

"Oh." I waited a few seconds. "I thought you were an astronaut."

He laughed again but stopped when the noise from outside got louder. I rolled down the window to hear what Chief Martin was saying to Dad.

I heard him say, "Old Herb...car...and baby. Not sure about the car. I think it's gonna blow!"

"Old Herb. Lydia. I know them."

I started to open the door, but Mr. McCool held my arm firmly.

"You're staying right here with me, dear."

I saw Dad yank his fireman's coat from off the truck, pick up a crowbar, and run toward the middle of everything.

Now that my eyes were getting used to the scene, I could see the blue car by a tree. There was a cloud of dust and smoke weaving overhead. Men surrounded the car, trying to pry open doors, bending low to look inside. With people shifting back and forth, I couldn't see what was going on. After a while, two men pulled away from the crowd carrying a stretcher.

I recognized Herb with his beard sticking out below the oxygen mask as they carried him to the ambulance. "That's Old Herb," I pointed out. With relief I saw Lydia and Deborah. They seemed to be all right, they were standing up. Another man followed the stretcher, carrying what appeared to be a leg with a boot still on the foot.

"Oh my God," Mr. McCool said, as he put his hand over my eyes. "I'm sorry." He made me put my head down.

"That's just his leg. He has a fake leg."

"You know this man?"

"Yeah. It's Old Herb Hoagland. That's his daughter's car."

"Herb from the elevator? I know him, from back when… What happened to his leg?"

"He had to have it amputated after he fell off the elevator roof."

"Poor man. I played cards with him."

I tried to raise my head.

"It's probably best you just stay down," he said.

"What do you see?" I asked. I wanted to look and I didn't want to look at the same time.

"Let me see." He hummed, tapping on the seat in front of him. "There is a baby. And now they're pulling out a woman. Your dad is carrying the baby. Now I can't see, too many people milling around. Now they're getting the woman on a stretcher and moving away from the car."

I remembered what the chief said. "They said it was going to blow. Is it going to blow up?"

"Well, I don't know. I guess they thought it might. Everyone is moving back now."

"Are they all right?"

"As far as I can see. You can be proud of your dad. He's the brave one. He's a hero, right there. He went right in there and helped them out of that car. And yes, it is on fire. Everyone's getting back."

"Can I look?"

Mr. McCool seemed to understand my curiosity. "I think so, now."

I looked up and saw my dad right there in the middle of all that action. He handed Bobby to Deborah and helped her to the ambulance. Then Dad put his arm around Lydia and walked her toward our car. We watched together in silence. I was watching all that goes on at the scene of a real emergency. Firemen were putting out the fire in the car. It didn't blow. My dad was right there, an important part.

As soon as the ambulance left for the hospital, siren screaming, Dad walked to the car with Lydia, who was cocooned in a blanket.

"Everybody's gonna be all right," Dad said. "Lydia's fine. She's coming home with us since everyone else went to the hospital. Turns out, they're all related to Herb Hoagland. From what I understand, they were driving home from town, bringing Herb with them to show him how they'd fixed up that church. The baby was crying and they were all talking or arguing or whatever in the car, and they didn't notice the train. It just caught the front bumper and they rolled over and crumpled up the doors and hit that tree."

"A miracle," said Mr. McCool.

Marty and Kristy came into view. I'd forgotten all about them and the stop sign. I looked toward the railroad crossing. Now that some of the cars were gone, I saw that the sign was there, a little crooked, but there. So Marty had been there and put up the sign before this happened. It wasn't in any way his fault.

I looked at Marty and cocked my head toward the stop sign. He nodded. Again we shared secret knowledge.

I turned to Kristy. "Why are you here?" She looked like a little child.

"I'll tell you later," Marty said.

"I'm freezing," Kristy said, arms folded around her body, definitely not dressed for this weather. She looked so ordinary standing there with her hair wet from the snow. Her eyes looked puffy like she'd been crying. I didn't think it was just from the cold.

We headed back to Grandma's. Dad put Lydia up front closer to the heater and I sat in back again with Mr. McCool. I leaned against him, suddenly tired, almost weak, like I'd stayed up all night or worked all day in the garden.

The Red Cross workers headed toward their barracks. Many lives were saved this day. The nurse leaned her weary head against the shoulder of Dr. McCool. The driver brought the truck to a stop.

"Wake up, Jude. We're here." Dad was calling me. I'd fallen asleep.

It was no longer snowing, breaks appeared in the clouds, stars showed through. The moon was a crescent, but somehow I wasn't afraid. Dad, Lydia, and I walked up to the house where light from the windows shone in blue ribbons across the snow. I looked up at the stars in their familiar patterns.

Grandma opened the door, and we entered the warmth of the living room. The twins ran to the door. "What happened, what happened?" Phil and Rita stood nearby, waiting for news.

"Everybody's going to be okay," Dad announced. "It was Herb Hoagland and his daughter and her family. Their car got nicked by the train. They took them to the hospital, looked like some minor injuries, but Lydia's fine. She's staying with one of us tonight."

Lana rushed to Lydia and put her arms around her. Rita smoothed Lydia's hair and said, "Let's go into the kitchen and get some cocoa."

"Dad was a hero," I said. "He pulled them out of a burning car." I looked at him, proud.

"Where's Marty?" Grandma looked around the room. "He never came back."

"Oh, he was there with us. He's fine. He should be right behind us."

"Well, we're certainly blessed." Grandma put her hand over her heart.

Mr. McCool came in next, followed by Marty and Kristy. He stamped his feet on the welcome mat. "All's well that ends well," he said.

"Let's go home," said Dad. "That's enough excitement for one day."

When our car pulled out of the driveway, I looked back at Grandma's house. Danny McCool was standing there in the middle of our family waving good-bye to us.

CHAPTER 23

November 1968

I WOKE UP AT TEN O'CLOCK THE NEXT MORNING, THANKSGIVING DAY. I slept late even though my curtains were open and the sun shone brightly into my room. I lay in bed remembering what it was like when Mom was alive. She always got up at five or six o'clock on Thanksgiving morning to put the turkey in the oven. A surge of roasted meat aromas always hit me halfway down the stairs. In the kitchen, Mom wore her apron with the turkey applique, orange Thanksgiving towels hung on the oven door, pies sat on the counter...

This year Thanksgiving dinner was going to be at Aunt Rita's house. Dad bought some rolls and coffee. Rita said that was all we needed to bring.

I went downstairs and it smelled like nothing. Dad was watching the Thanksgiving parade on TV and drinking coffee. I took a bowl out of the dish drainer and filled it with Cheerios, the only cereal we had left. Marty was not up yet. Kristy was asleep on the couch in the den. Lydia spent the night with Lana. I couldn't say we were back to normal, but at least the excitement from last night was over.

It turned out that Kristy's life was not so perfect after all.

When we got home from Grandma Walstra's the night before, we wrapped Kristy in Dad's bathrobe and parked her at our kitchen table. She looked like an orphaned child. I left her there to warm up by the heating vent and followed Marty upstairs while Dad called Kristy's mom and dad to let them know what happened.

Marty stood in his bedroom in sweatpants and sweatshirt, a pile of wet clothes at his feet.

"She made me take her," he said. "She was at the house when I got there."

"How'd she know?"

"Eddie told her."

"How?"

"She used to go with us sometimes."

"Why'd you take her and not me?"

"She just came with Brad. I don't know."

"That's not fair."

"Listen, Eddie told her I was returning the stuff right then. She was there when I got to the house. She ran all the way from her house, said her parents were arguing about Brad. Her mom's looney. So she wanted me to take her in the truck. I didn't want to, Jude. I think she's got a crush on me or something. But I couldn't just leave her there. I had to take those signs."

"You could have taken her home."

"She cried and said she didn't want to go there. I didn't know what to do with her. Anyway, she helped me. She helped hold the stop sign up, while I put the screws in. Then we took the others out to the highway department, and I thought since she was so upset it would be best to just bring her back with me. She's your friend, right? I thought maybe you or Dad could help her. I didn't know what to do with her."

I don't think Marty had ever talked to me so much at one time.

"I better go down and see how she is," I said.

Downstairs, Dad told me Kristy's mom was having some kind of problem, some kind of meltdown. Kristy would stay with us for Thanksgiving because her dad was taking her mom to the doctor and they'd be in Fort Wayne over Thanksgiving.

By the time we were all dressed and made it to Aunt Rita's, it was almost time to eat. We gathered 'round the holiday table. Rita's best china plate settings and crystal glasses sat on a lace tablecloth surrounding a centerpiece of Indian corn and glowing orange candles. I scanned the faces around me. Besides Dad, me, Marty, Rita, Phil, Lana, the twins, and Grandma, there were the McCools and Lydia and Kristy. I thought it was a strange mixture of people, but that's just how it turned out. Kristy was wearing my blue shirt and jeans because hers were in the wash. Dressed in my clothes, she seemed as ordinary as the rest of us, plus I realized now that she had problems in her life, too.

Aunt Rita set the turkey in front of Uncle Phil, wiped her face with a kitchen towel, and sat down. Everyone else sat down, and Dad prayed a short prayer thanking God for the food and for blessing us all. Then we ate.

Late that afternoon, the McCools left for Indianapolis. We waved from the front door and watched their black Buick until it turned at the end of the road and was gone.

EPILOGUE

November 1982

THAT THANKSGIVING WAS FOURTEEN YEARS AGO. I WISH I COULD SAY that what I learned that summer and fall would enable me to sail through the following years without any trouble, but that wouldn't be true. When I hit junior high, it was just like Trudy said. It was the pits. I had to start all over again making friends and fitting in. I think even Kristy might have had some trouble, but I'll never know since her family moved back to Fort Wayne before the end of the school year and the *Glass House* was empty again.

The little country church was empty again, too, within a couple of years. The only reason the Mayhughs had lived there in the first place was because Old Herb had arranged it. They were his family. He said his own house wasn't fit for kids, and he didn't think he could stand having a baby and so many people around, family or not. He was used to being alone. But it turns out Old Herb did have some money, and it was Danny McCool who came up with the idea to remodel his old house so the Mayhughs could live there, too. They remodeled it so it was like two apartments, and my dad did most of the work. Now, all of that didn't happen overnight, but when Danny McCool first suggested it at the Thanksgiving table, nobody thought it could happen at all.

So much serendipity, so much of God working in mysterious ways.

I did go to college—with a little money from Grandma Walstra, an academic scholarship, and encouragement from Daniel McCool. I earned degrees in creative writing and journalism at Purdue University...and I'm getting ready to write that mystery novel.

To order additional copies of

The Bright Side of the Moon

have your credit card ready and call
1 800-917-BOOK (2665)

or e-mail
orders@selahbooks.com

or order online at
www.selahbooks.com

CPSIA information can be obtained
at www.ICGtesting.com
Printed in the USA
FFOW01n1443071214
9235FF